THE NOT SO LITTLE MERMAN

THE SILVER ISLES: BOOK TWO

C.W. GRAY

TANGLEWOOD PRESS

❀ Created with Vellum

The rain pounded against the window panes of Dover's cozy home. Kit empathized with the glass. It seemed like life suddenly wanted to drown him in a storm of decisions and change.

"I don't want to live in the Northern Silver Isles." His head thumped against the back of his chair. "You and Kai are here, and I'm actually starting to like our parents."

His brother, Dover, watched him from his spot on the sofa, a bowl of chowder propped on his large, pregnant belly. His otter companion, Chubber, stretched out along the back of the sofa, snoring loudly.

Dover ate the last spoonful of clam chowder in his bowl before speaking. "Father won't force you to marry him, Kit, you know that. Talk to him and tell him you're not going to do it. Prince Tack is nice and all, but with the curse, you'll never have a physical relationship."

For months now, the northern king had been in negotiations with Kit's father to create a marriage contract between Kit and Prince Tack. King Nerio and Prince Tack were both forces of nature and wouldn't back down. They wanted the alliance with the Southern Silver Isles, and for some reason, in their eyes, only a marriage to Kit would be acceptable.

Dover gave him a sad look and held up his empty bowl.

Kit took it and refilled it from the large pot on the stove. "Preggo hunger is a real thing, Dover. I'll take care of you." When Kit was pregnant with Pearl, he was hungry all the time too.

He'd always loved food and had the belly to prove it. Unfortunately, pregnancy hadn't exactly helped him lose that extra thirty pounds his mother insisted he needed to work on.

Dover started in on the new bowl. His dog, Otis, hovered next to the sofa, hoping for a bite. *You're out of luck, buddy*, Kit thought with a smile. His youngest brother really liked chowder.

Dover looked up, licking a bit of chowder from the corner of his mouth. "One of the others would step up. Lorelei wants to be a queen."

Kit scowled. His stupid sister didn't even like the prince. She just wanted to be chosen over all their other sisters and brothers. He may not know Prince Tack well, but he wouldn't wish his sister on the man. For fuck's sake, the Muir family was already cursed. They didn't need Lorelei on top of that.

Kit breathed out, shoulders slumping. "It doesn't matter. Prince Tack told Father he will only marry me. I think it's because I have Pearl. He knows I'm fertile."

Dover swallowed a bite and eyed him. "But you can't have sex."

"I'll be artificially inseminated," Kit replied with a shrug.

Prince Tack's curse ensured he couldn't touch any other living being without causing them unbearable pain. That didn't mean science couldn't work around the curse to make sure Tack's bloodline continued.

"I know that." Dover rolled his eyes. "I mean you'll never be able to have sex with your husband. What kind of marriage is that?"

Kit gave him a flat look. "Sex is just one aspect of a relationship, Dover, and it doesn't have to be the most important one. I can deal with that. I'm used to going without anyway."

Honestly, the idea of having someone of his own, sex or no sex, appealed to him. The only problem was that he didn't see Prince Tack agreeing to cuddle up on the couch to watch a movie. The man had a cold air swirling about him that kept everyone in the southern court at a distance.

Not that anyone would want to befriend a Coalswell.

"Is it the artificial insemination?" Dover frowned. "It seems so emotionless."

"No," Kit said, propping his chin on his fist. "It's just one way to get pregnant, and I'll admit I like the idea of more babies. Pearl will be a good big sister."

"Then what is it, Kit?" Dover asked. "This marriage will ease the tension between our kingdoms. We've all been fully prepared to make a political marriage. If I hadn't heard the mating call, I would have expected it too."

Kit had known he would be married off one day, in theory, but after he participated in the heat swarm and got pregnant with Pearl, his mother had given up on marrying him off.

Until the prince of the fucking Northern Silver Isles insisted on marrying me.

"It's not the marriage itself. It's the moving to the Northern Silver Isles part." Kit shuddered. "I've heard stories. Coalswell Tides is supposed to be a horrible, cold place full of unhappy, impoverished people. They're basically pirates, Dover, and I hear King Nerio and Prince Tack horde any treasure they find, leaving their people to starve."

How could Pearl and I possibly be happy in such a place?

He reached down to pet Otis. Dover's dog was a sweet boy.

Dover tilted his head. "Aren't pirates supposed to be sexy?"

Kit snorted. "They're murderers and have scurvy. Not. Sexy."

Dover laughed. "Okay, good point." He gave Kit a serious look. "I think you're wrong about them though. They seemed nice enough when I met them."

Kit arched a brow. "Yes, he did refrain from kidnapping you and using you for political leverage."

Dover made a face. "Exactly. He *didn't* do that.

Instead, he offered Ben and I a safe place if father exiled us."

"Maybe he wanted to make you clean their hordes of treasure while watching them eat all the food in the kingdom."

Dover arched his brow again.

"Okay." Kit chuckled. "That's a bit ridiculous."

"Just a little."

Kit was quiet for a moment. He thought about the negotiations. "Prince Tack agreed to let me stay here until I conceived," he admitted. "I didn't expect that." He hadn't expected the prince to compromise, period. He sure wasn't budging on anything else.

"I don't know what to tell you, Kit." Dover set down his empty bowl. "This is a decision *you* have to make for yourself."

Kit groaned and collapsed on the sofa, then pressed his head to Dover's belly. "When did you become so sensible? Remember when you ran from all your troubles and worries?"

Dover laughed, shaking Kit's head with the movement. "Finding my mate, adopting a tentacle tailed baby, and getting pregnant made me grow up. Who would have thought it?"

Kit smiled up at his brother. "I'm proud of you, irmãozinho. You've become a strong voice for the guppy tails."

Dover flushed. "You and your fancy endearments. It's not that big of a deal. I'm just finally doing what I should have done a long time ago."

Kit smiled again, then sat up. "I better get home.

Fergus and Pearl will be back from the beach soon."

Dover held out his hands and Kit helped him off the couch. "How are you handling father, mother, and Fergus?"

Not too long ago, King Ren had shocked his court by revealing he had not one, but two mates – Queen Kelby and their ever-loyal servant, Fergus. That had been hard for many to accept, but Kit's parents had added to the uproar by explaining that six of King Ren's thirteen children were Fergus's.

Kit scrunched his nose. "You love him already, don't you? The two of you were already on good terms before we found out he's your omega father."

Dover cupped his cheek and held him still. "He's your father too, Kit. Me, you, Kai, Eugenia, Reif, and Mabella are all his."

Kit swallowed. "It's hard. Mother and I have never had an easy relationship, but she was our mother. Father was a distant authority figure, and Mother was a critical social butterfly. As much as I didn't like it, those were certainties. Now, I don't know anything."

Dover hugged him. "Change isn't easy, but these changes are for the better. Father and his mates are happy now. They can live and love one another in the open. We'll adapt as everything settles."

Kit squeezed Dover tight, then let him go. "There's the crux of my problem. I won't be here for that, remember?"

Dover whimpered and buried his face against Kit's neck. "Damn it. I'll miss you."

They hugged for a few more moments, then Kit

forced himself to let Dover go. "I really should go. I'll bring Pearl by in the morning to play with Shawn."

"Okay. Love you."

"Love you too." Kit kissed Dover's cheek, then left.

Outside, he skirted a wide path around Ben's chicken, Rachael. The beast glared at him from her perch on the covered porch. *Human pets are so strange.*

The rain was a familiar comfort as it fell on his face and bare chest. It never got too cold in the Southern Silver Isles, but they did get a lengthy wet season. Fortunately, it was almost over.

Coalswell Tides was supposed to be a frozen block of ice and snow. *I don't want to have to wear more than a sarong*, he thought.

He scowled at himself, then ruffled his red curls. "Think positive, Kit. You always wanted to get one of those winter hats with the little fox ears. Now's the time."

He reached the base of Dover's waterfall and walked up the steps carved into the steep cliff. At the top, he waded into the swollen river and shifted, summoning his clownfish tail.

He fought the current for a moment and enjoyed the refreshing water rushing over his body. The castle was home, but it was also full of drama and intrigue. He loved his family, even Lorelei, but it would be nice to have a place of his own. He envied Dover his creek and waterfall.

Kit slowly swam to where Dover's creek joined a larger branch of the main river. Where Dover's creek had very little traffic, the larger tributaries leading to the main river were full of merfolk hurrying about their business. They swam below while boats traveled above, moving goods to and from Latch Bay.

A few miles later, Kit stopped for a quick break. Clownfish tails were quite a bit shorter than some, and Kit was getting a little tired. He studied the swaying river grass and the sandy river bottom. *I wonder what kind of waterways the Northern Silver Isles has.*

His attention caught on the colorful contrast of his bright yellow sarong against his orange, white, and black tail. "I'll still wear yellow when I live on the iceberg."

A long, brown shark tail caught his eye before he was yanked into a hug. "Why are you talking to yourself?" Kai asked.

Kit's twin brother looked absolutely nothing like him. He had a tiger shark tail, thick brown hair, and a bunch of muscles.

"I thought I was alone." Kit flushed when he noticed more mers taking their own breaks around him.

Kai laughed and let Kit go. "You're the least observant mer in the Silver Isles."

Kit rolled his eyes and started swimming again. "Don't remind me. Not everyone can be perfect warriors like you and Talia."

Kai winced. "Fuck. Has Lorelei been giving you trouble again?"

"Her existence troubles me." Kit swished his tail angrily, trying to keep up with Kai's faster movement. "Why is she such a snotty pain in the ass? I swear if I hear one more comment about my fat ass –"

"She said that?" Kai growled, hand moving to rest on the spear strapped to his back. "I never heard her say that."

Kit shook his head, laughing. "That's because she knows you or Talia will kick her butt. What are you going to do? Stab her for telling me my ass is fat?"

"Maybe." Kai pouted. "She wouldn't call you fat again."

Kit snickered. "True."

"Now, what was all that about living on an iceberg?"

Kit's amusement drained away. "I'm thinking about going through with the marriage to Prince Tack."

Kai scowled. "We can't trust the damned Coalswells. They have to have some ulterior motive."

Kit snorted. "I won't get them the southern throne. Father has already made it clear that if the marriage happens, I forfeit my title and right to the throne."

Kai eyed him. "How do you feel about that?"

Kit shrugged. It always disturbed him to think he was third in line to inherit the throne. "Don't want to be king anyway. I'd much rather Talia or you rule."

His brother shuddered. "Just Talia. I'd probably murder half the court if they put me in charge."

Kit laughed. "No, you wouldn't. You'd be a good king."

Kai flushed and looked away. "Ruling isn't what I want. I just want to stay here so I can watch Talia's back."

"Why wouldn't you be here?" Kit frowned. Kai almost looked sad.

Kai looked around before swimming closer. "I

haven't told anyone, but I met my mate. He's from the Deep."

Kit's mouth fell open. "Seriously?"

His brother nodded, shoulders slumping. "Obviously, that isn't going to work out, but I've been trying to come to terms with it."

"You've always dreamed of a true mating," Kit whispered, grabbing Kai's hand.

As tough and brash as Kai was, he was a squishy romantic too.

"Dreams are all they'll be." Kai looked away. "It was a selfish dream anyway. My duty is protecting Latch Bay."

"I'm so sorry." Kit frowned. "Wait, why won't a mating to a tentacle tail work? Now that father is more accepting, he wouldn't forbid it. Also, Sea Witch Johanna isn't as bad as we thought she'd be. Your mate could come live –"

"No!" Kai's tone left no room for argument. "That's not an option. He wants nothing to do with me and he's as tied to the Deep as I am to the Southern Silver Isles. My loyalty is to my family, not some stranger. There is no fixing it, Kit. Just let it alone."

Kit rested his head on Kai's shoulder as they approached the bay. "Okay. I'm here for you, though, alright? Even if I'm living on an iceberg, I'm only a call away."

"Do they even have phones in Coalswell Tides?" Kai gave him a teasing smile.

"Oh, shut up." Kit shoved him and swam away,

sighing when Kai easily caught up to him. "I guess I'll do it. I'll marry the damn northern prince."

CHAPTER 2

A few weeks later, Kit fiddled with the emerald green armband he wore. "Isn't this a bit fast?" he asked Dover. They stood together in front of the large mirror in the changing room. "I've only spoken to Prince Tack three times. Three *brief* times."

Queen Kelby pushed into Dover's space before he could answer. She straightened the green and gold strand of beads he wore at his right temple, then stilled his fingers on his armband. "Stop fidgeting, dear. Unfortunately, the Coalswells want this to happen quickly. It's unseemly, but they *are* the Coalswells."

"It's not a big deal, just fast." He forced a smile.

"If this were my wedding, it would be at one of the island estates to the west," Lorelei said, brushing her golden hair. "It would be a private affair with only the most prominent aristocratic mers of the court allowed."

"Ah, but the northern prince didn't want you, did he?" Dover smirked, clasping his hands over his swollen belly. "Looks like you'll always just be a princess."

Lorelei's eyes narrowed to slits and Kit thought she'd start hissing soon.

Talia clapped her hands to get their attention. "That's enough, you two. Today is about Kit." She held up Kit's crown and carried it to him. His crown was a gold diadem covered in saltwater pearls and tiny, white tulip shells. It had eight gently sloped points, each holding a small teardrop emerald.

"You look pretty, Daddy." Pearl bounced in place and grinned.

He smiled softly. "You look pretty too, baby girl."

Pearl had just turned three and was growing like seagrass.

"You've never looked more regal." Fergus stood behind Pearl, eyes soft with emotion.

"That's the truth," Lorelei snorted.

Dover shoved her and she glared at him.

"Watch it, guppy prince."

Dover narrowed his eyes. "Stop being such a narcissistic twat."

Enough!" Talia demanded as she stepped between them and ended the fight with one stern look.

A rush of longing hit Kit hard. "I wanted more time here," he blurted out. "I wanted more time with all of you."

Eugenia gave him a surprised look. "Really? I'd give millions to get away from them."

"Eugenia." Kelby glared, scolding his sister. "We're your family."

Eugenia rolled her eyes. "I didn't say I didn't love you. You all are just really annoying. Besides, Kit isn't dying." Eugenia tossed a pillow at him. It hit his bare chest and fell to the floor. "We'll come visit you in the frozen pits of Coalswell Tides."

"Oh hush, Eugenia." Kelby adjusted the knot of his green and gold sarong. "I'm sure it's a pleasant place."

Lorelei applied another coat of lipstick. "I hear the king's father went insane and they had to lock him in a cellar."

"Lorelei!" Kelby looked appalled. "Enough. What has gotten into you all today? We are royalty and should act like it."

"I hear they're all shark tailed merfolk and they eat any mer that doesn't have the right tail," Eugenia whispered against his ear. "The royal family feeds the innocent to their pet monsters."

Kelby groaned and pushed Eugenia and Lorelei toward the door. "You two get out. Go wait at the entrance."

"Mother, I still have to get dressed." Lorelei sniffed and grabbed her pink sarong. "Give us a minute."

Kelby glared at them. "Just keep quiet."

Kai twirled one of his daggers. "I suggested letting me stab them, but Kit said *No, we can't do that*."

"Unki Kai, you're so funny," Pearl giggled.

"He is, sweetness." Fergus shook his head. "Now, don't you have something to give your daddy?"

"Oh yeah." Her eyes brightened and she ran over to hand him the square box she carried. "A damned Coalswell gave it to me."

They all turned to glare at Kai.

He gave them an innocent look and shrugged. "What? She could have heard that anywhere."

"He said it was for you, Daddy." Pearl danced in place, her pretty yellow dress bouncing as she moved.

Kai shrugged and opened the box. His eyes widened when he saw the necklace inside. "Holy shellfish."

Lorelei was by his side in an instant. "That's a Napoleonic-era diamond and emerald necklace. It had to have cost millions."

"Am I supposed to wear it?" Kit asked, blinking. "I guess it would match."

"You don't deserve that necklace." Lorelei snarled and grabbed the box.

"For fuck's sake,, Lorelei." Talia grabbed Lorelei's shoulders and shook her. "Calm your ass down and get dressed."

Lorelei growled but tossed the box to Kit. "I hate you so much right now."

About an hour later, he watched Lorelei direct Pearl and her flower basket down the aisle. She giggled when Pearl did a bouncy little dance before starting down the aisle.

He sighed. "As much as I dislike her, Lorelei is a good aunt."

"I'm better." Eugenia winked as she passed him.

Dover stuck his tongue out at Eugenia's back. "I'm better than all of them."

Kai gave Dover an annoyed look. "Fuck you. I'm the best uncle."

"Pearl loves *each* of you," Kit said with a smile.

Talia pushed Dover and Kai out the door, then turned to hug him. "Thank you for doing this, Kit. I know what you're sacrificing for our kingdom, and I will always be here for you, no matter where you live."

Kit blinked away his tears and watched as each of his siblings filed down the center of the decorated ballroom, dressed in their nicest jewelry and most expensive sarongs.

He closed his eyes and focused on the rain falling against the windows. He could barely hear it with the wedding music playing. *This is for the good of the kingdom. We don't want another clash with the Northern Silver Isles. Father just broke his curse and deserves some peace.*

"Son?" King Ren stood on one side of him. "Are you sure you want to do this?"

"If not, we'll find another way." Fergus stood on his other side.

Kit took Fergus's hand and squeezed it. "I just wish I had more time with you. I feel like I'm only now getting used to the idea of you as my omega father."

"I'll always be here for you." Fergus kissed his hand.

Ren took his other hand. "As will Kelby and I. We love you, Kit."

Kit's eyes watered again. He had waited his whole life to hear those words from his alpha father. They fell more easily from Ren's lips now that the curse was broken, but the king was still awkward in showing his affection. The curse had been much more ingrained in Ren than in any of his children.

"Are you ready?" Ren asked.

Kit nodded, then it was time to go. His fathers walked him down the aisle of the packed ballroom. There were very few Coalswells there, and Queen Kelby had *forgotten* to invite the Sea Witch or her apprentice.

I should be relieved, but I kinda like Sea Witch Johanna, he thought.

Every aristocratic mer of the Southern Silver Isles was in attendance, but so were many of his newer guppy tailed friends.

Shauna and Nami smiled encouragingly as he passed. Nami's mate, Eloise, wiggled her brows and blew him a kiss, making him roll his eyes. Romeu, a crocodile shifter, and his wife sat with all of their children. Joy patted at her eyes and sniffled. She had told Kit she always cried at weddings.

As he reached the front, he smiled softly when he saw his mother sitting with little Shawn in her lap. Ben and Dover's adopted son had completely stolen all their hearts, tentacle tail and all.

Kit pressed his lips together to hide his laughter when he saw Sea Witch Johanna sitting beside Kelby. She gave him a mischievous look and wiggled her fingers in greeting.

Dover's mate, Ben, sat beside her. He crossed his eyes and made a face when Kit passed him. Kit snickered and shook his head. Dover's human was as strange as his chicken.

Kit's attention caught on the black clothed figures at the front of the room, surrounded by his family. King Nerio and Prince Tack looked eerily alike. They both had tan faces, dark hair and dark eyes. They wore black from the neck down and no jewelry except their burnished gold crowns, darkened with age and covered in musgravite gems and dark seashells.

Kit swallowed hard when Prince Tack's eyes met his. The prince's face remained expressionless, but those dark eyes sent a shiver down Kit's back.

Ren patted Kit's hand, then moved to stand beside King Nerio. Both kings would perform the wedding ceremony.

Fergus kissed his cheek, then whispered in his ear. "Remember, treasure isn't always obvious to the eye. That necklace sure is pretty, but you may be gaining far more then fine jewelry today."

Kit gave his father a thoughtful look, then turned and moved closer to Prince Tack's side. Together they faced the two kings.

Kit almost jumped when Tack's gloved hand took his. He could feel the heat of the other man's skin through the soft material. Kit's heart beat fast. He gently squeezed Tack's fingers.

Ren held his hands up. "Today, before the Goddess and the sea, we join together the Rees and Muir families."

CHAPTER 3

THREE MONTHS LATER

*T*ack rubbed the bridge of his nose. "Okay. Dad, the book says lying to your kids is a sure way to mess them up. Do they mean lying about something like Santa Claus or lying about having just fed a pirate to Lola? Those would both be good lies, right?"

His father looked up from the piles of paperwork on his desk. "Did you feed another pirate to Lola? Son, you really need to stop doing that. We have a bad reputation already, but you and your friends make it worse when you do things like that."

Tack shrugged. "I didn't *really* feed him to her. I just didn't tell her *not* to eat him. You know Lola doesn't like the taste of people anyway. She spit him right back out."

"Tack." Nerio groaned and rubbed his face. "What am I going to do with you?"

"Answer my question." Tack waved the book on

child care at his father. "What does it mean when it says not to lie to your kids?"

"For the love of... It probably means to be as honest as possible." Nerio sighed. "Don't avoid the hard discussions by making things up. Remember when Tilda passed away?"

Tack nodded. Losing his childhood nanny had hurt. Tilda hadn't been able to physically touch him, but she had found ways to make sure he knew he was loved.

"You were six, but I didn't tell you she moved away or anything, did I?"

"No." Tack tilted his head in thought. "You said she had been sick for a long time. She died so her soul could return to the sea and she could be at peace."

"That's what that book of yours is talking about." Nerio shook his head. "I should have Petra toss them out. They do nothing but make you worry. You'll be a good father."

Tack scowled and set the book back on top of the stack next to him. "I need to be ready for when Kit and Pearl come home."

Nerio's eyes softened. "Son, are you sure this is the best choice?"

Tack's eyes narrowed. "Absolutely. He's my mate."

"Yes, but he doesn't know that." Nerio gave him a thoughtful look. "I would say you should simply tell him, but that tactic didn't work out well for Fin."

Tack looked out the leaded glass of the study window. Just as it had for over a thousand years, the thick Coalswell forest guarded the upper keep of Muir Castle.

The leaves of the Coalswell Oak trees were so dark a green they almost looked black, but the forest was alive with movement and color. Summer was a busy time for the gnomes, fairies, and wood sprites that lived within it.

Tack leaned back in his chair and watched the gently swaying trees. *What will Kit think of it here? It's so different from the Southern Silver Isles.* The gold band on his finger was a constant reminder of his responsibility to his new husband. It was also a continuous reminder of Tack's connection to the man he loved. *I have to ensure he's happy here.*

"Son?"

Tack turned his attention back to his father. "I can't simply forget him, Dad. Maybe if he was happy, I could let things be, but he's not. I saw it in his eyes the day we met."

Nerio gave him a sad look. "Tack, you've only spoken to him a few times. How can you possibly know if he's happy or not?"

Tack shook his head. "He's alone there. With as many brothers and sisters as he has, he doesn't quite fit in with them, and he knows it. He has only a few people to confide in, and they're all busy with their own lives. He needs a person of his own, someone to guard his back and watch out for him."

"I see. You'll try to break the curse, then?" Nerio looked grim. Tack couldn't exactly blame him.

"No." Tack swallowed hard and picked up another book. "Each time a person of our bloodline tries to break the curse, it ends disastrously. I just want to make Kit happy. If I get a small piece of him in the process, I'm a selfish enough bastard to be glad for it."

Nerio gave him a hard look. "You aren't your uncle, and Kit isn't Victoria. Are you sure you won't try?"

Tack's mouth twitched, and he couldn't prevent his half-smile. "What about you, Dad? Don't think I haven't noticed a few changes in your behavior. Are you keen on trying to hunt down your mate?"

Nerio blushed and cleared his throat. "Enough of that. What do you make of Ailig's attack on Laird Marcel's lands?"

Tack scowled. "He's escalating. He recruits more pirates every day, and they're getting more brazen. This wasn't just an attack on one of our merchant ships or excavation teams. Marcel barely pushed them back."

Nerio leaned back in his chair, bracing his elbows on his chair arms and linking his fingers together. "We can't find his base of operations, but it must be close to the isles. Hali is searching, but there is absolutely no trace to follow."

Tack scowled. That had been the case for the past two years. The isles weren't *that* big. They should have found Ailig and his pirates months ago.

"Did she tell you what she heard?" Tack asked, tracing the title of the book he held, *Becoming a Step-Father*.

"Rumor is he's working with someone." Nerio scowled. "Someone with more money and manpower."

"It's not King Ren." Tack set the book aside. "I haven't spent much time at his court, but he's sincere in wanting peace between us."

Nerio didn't look convinced. "So, he says. I've known the man a lot longer than you. He was a cold-hearted son of a bitch before his curse broke. I'm not sure I believe he's changed so much."

The door opening interrupted their conversation. Petra's smiling face greeted them. The castle steward was covered in mud and looked exhausted despite her good mood.

She bowed deeply. "My most honored King and Prince of the Northern Silver Isles, Prince Kit's garden is finished."

Tack jumped up, heading for the door. "Perfect. I want everything in place before he gets here."

"And his attention is gone again." Nerio stood slowly. "Petra, you look like you need a nap. Hell, you almost sound deferential." He shuddered. "It creeps me out."

The merwoman laughed. "I've been working some long fucking days to finish this up for Tack. His tropical prince better appreciate it."

"Why didn't you let the groundskeepers handle it? You need to learn not to micromanage." Nerio sniffed. "You smell horrible."

Tack heard Petra punch Nerio's arm and winced. He quickly left them behind and hurried down the hall. The castle was massive, with several levels and expansive grounds. It was also ancient. Each new generation added on to it, and they all tried to match the style of the same concentric stone castle Tack's ancestors had built when they migrated here from the Irish Sea.

Since merfolk were of the land and sea and needed easy access to both, the main keep stood atop a high cliff but extended over and down the cliff and into the stormy Coalswell Sea. Tack had quarters in both the upper and lower castle. *I wonder which Kit will prefer.*

Tack skidded around a corner and ran into his best friend, Finch. Tack grabbed his arm when Finch stumbled and almost fell.

"Where the hell are you going in such a rush? Are we under attack?" Finch arched a brow and straightened up. The Kelpie was the epitome of dark seduction from his caramel skin to his soulful black eyes. He was also a pain in the ass.

"Kit's garden is ready." Tack pushed past him.

"Sweet." Finch jogged beside him. "I got to see this. You've had Petra and her crew working on it for six months. I can't believe you've gone to all this trouble for an arranged marriage."

"Fuck off." He turned another corner and ran into his cousins. "Damn it, why is everyone in the way?"

Hali arched a brow. "Oh no. Are we inconveniencing our crown prince with our existence?"

Her brother, Seamus, snickered. "What lit a fire up your ass, Tack?"

Tack scowled and ignored them, finally reaching the end of the royal wing of the main keep. The wide double doors leading to Kit's garden had remained closed for months. Now, they stood open.

"Did Petra finally finish your over the top, way too

high maintenance wedding gift?" Hali asked from behind him.

"Oh, hush, Hali." Seamus nudged his sister with his shoulder. "I think it's sweet."

Tack went through the doors and looked around. A massive saltwater pool with a fifty-foot waterfall covering six acres dominated the enclosed garden. Around it, Petra had created a tropical paradise protected by thick-paned, well-insulated glass and heated lights.

"Holy whale spouts, this is beautiful," Hali said, awe filling her voice.

"How much did this cost again?" Seamus asked. "Shit, you'll need a full staff to maintain this, Tack."

"I have plenty of money to spend." Tack slipped his boots off and waded into the pool, summoning his Great White shark tail as the water deepened.

Finch shucked his clothes and ran into the water, shifting into his horse form as he went.

Together, they explored the depths of the pool. The bottom was sandy and seagrass swayed in the artificial current. Seashells mixed with decorative stones and starfish and a hermit crab crawled below him.

Petra had created an artificial reef at the center of the pool and small, non-predatory tropical fish swam around, making themselves at home.

A water sprite peeked out of two twisted bits of coral and giggled. Her delicate, translucent face was full of mischief.

Finch nudged her with his snout and she patted his nose before swimming away.

C.W. GRAY

Tack carefully inspected every inch of the pool. *It has to be perfect for Kit and Pearl.* He knew they were leaving their beloved reef behind, and the waters in the Northern Silver Isles were much harsher and more dangerous than in the south. Then there were the sharks.

Lola and the other sharks patrolled the lower castle grounds, and Kit and Pearl weren't familiar with the sharks and their special bond with Tack's people. It would take time for them to adjust.

Seamus floated past him, his stubby seal tail moving slowly. "Okay, Kit's garden is my favorite place now."

Hali swam past them quickly, the hind flippers of her own seal tail shooting her around the reef. "The water's too warm."

"It's not meant for you." Tack swiped at her with his gloved hand. "Kit and Pearl are used to warmer waters."

"They'll like this." Seamus sped up and chased after Hali. "If they don't, then I'll accept it as a favorite cousin present."

Tack snorted and watched a small sea turtle swim past him. "There are three doors. One on the main floor of the royal wing, another from our personal quarters, and the last toward the back for the gardeners. I'll need a minimum of two guards on each at all times."

He looked around for Finch. His friend was in charge of the Coalswell guard and would need to step up security around the castle.

26

Finch swam past Tack, slapping him on the back with his tail and neighing.

Tack glared at him. "A simple nod would have worked."

Hali snickered as she zipped past him again. "I bet you're going to double the guard when you have to lead an excavation."

He winced and chased after her, his long tail gliding through the water. "Actually, I need to talk to you about that."

Hali gave him a curious look. "Yeah?"

"I'll need to stay closer to home from now on. You've been leading excavations yourself for the past year. Would you mind taking on more?"

Hali stopped swimming, mouth falling open. Seamus and Finch also stopped swimming to stare at him.

He rolled his eyes when the little water sprite also gave him a disbelieving look. "What?"

"You *always* lead the excavations." Hali shook her head. "The only time I lead is when you're already doing another."

"You're hardly ever home," Seamus added. "You spend more time out in the open ocean than in the Coalswell Sea."

Finch gave a rude bray and shook his head.

Tack sighed. "I don't understand why I have to explain this to you since it should be apparent, but as a husband and father, I'll have a responsibility to my family. I need to be here for them. I'll still handle the excavations that are close to home, but I'd like Hali to take on the ones farther away."

Hali's cheeks puffed out as she tried not to laugh. "Family man."

Seamus covered his own smile, eyes dancing with laughter. "You're too adorable. I love it."

Finch leaned to the side and nibbled on some of the seagrass until the water sprite swatted at him. She started chasing Finch around the reef, and Hali and Seamus joined in, laughing as they swam.

Tack turned back to his inspection of Kit's garden. *Everything has to be perfect.*

CHAPTER 4

A few days later, he swam through the cold, open ocean with Lola, Hali, and a large excavation team. A shipwreck had been found in the Newfoundland Basin, and based on the pictures, Tack thought it might be a sunken Spanish Galleon, the Día Precioso. The ship had been lost at sea in 1638 and had carried a large quantity of silver, gold, and precious gems.

Tack eyed the dark waters around them, his gloved hand stroking Lola's side to check for tension. She was the best lookout he knew and they were all on edge after the attack on Laird Marcel.

"How did Declan even find it?" Hali asked. His cousin was the only seal tailed mer on the team, but each of them knew she could handle herself well. Even Lola refused to eye her hungrily and she loved seals.

Of course, Hali's Orca companion may have had something to do with that too. Cecilia swam below Hali.

"Metal detector." Tack shot her a grin. "Dec and Jamalla have started using them, and they've found more shipwrecks than the other scouts combined over the past year."

"Why didn't we think of that?" Harley asked. Tack's friend swam below him with his companion, a tiger shark named Daryl.

Tack gave him a considering look. "Do you want to suggest using modern technology to the elder scouts?"

Harley winced, his tiger shark tail swishing in agitation. "Hell, no."

Hali looked thoughtful. "It's times like this I think we cling too tightly to our traditions."

"Bah, that's nonsense." Dougal, one of the elder scouts, nudged Hali with his shoulder. "We've been plenty successful finding wrecks without all that modern shit getting in the way. I remember working plenty of big discoveries with both your fathers. Finbar always had a way of finding the best treasures."

Hali smiled softly. "He talks about it sometimes. I wish he'd come with us again."

Dougal's smile faded and he gave her a sad look. "You and me both, pup."

Tack rolled his wedding band around his finger. He wore it under his ever-present gloves, but the weight soothed him. *I won't make the same mistake Uncle Fin did.*

A few miles more, and they found Declan. The dolphin tailed merman swam in excited circles around what looked to be the barest outline of a large ship.

"Look it, Prince Tack! I started excavating the

borders while I waited. It's Spanish, for sure." Declan grinned wide. "Maybe we'll get lucky."

Declan's two dolphin companions, Chirp and Dahlia, circled Lola and Tack. He shot Lola a warning look, then reached out to greet the two playful creatures, stroking their noses and giving them plenty of pats. "Hey, you two. Good job leading Dec here."

"Ha." Declan back rolled over and over as he spoke. "Those two were useless. They just wanted to chase fish."

Lola bumped Tack's shoulder and he made sure to stroke her dorsal fin. "Don't eat me. You're still my favorite girl." He turned back to the others. "I have a good feeling about this one. Let's secure the perimeter and set up the equipment. I want to see what we have here."

Hours later, they had their camp set up, and the sharks were patrolling the area while Tack and the others surveyed the wreak, laying down metal grids to mark the boundaries.

Despite what many thought about the Coalswells, they were well trained and took the utmost care to preserve any archaeological finds they came across. A full excavation would take months, if not years.

Tack studied the layout of the parts they had found. The mystery of the Día Precioso had haunted the world for hundreds of years. In addition to its costly cargo, it had carried over a hundred passengers on their way to a new home.

He considered the location for a moment. In the

early and middle seventeen hundred's, the Newfoundland Basin had been crawling with sirens. The seductive creatures were known for their voracious appetites. They had often sung a ship to crash upon their rocks so they could feast on the crew and passengers.

The Northern Silver Isles had been covered in sirens when Tack's ancestors had arrived. Fortunately, merfolk were immune to their songs. Now, there was only a small colony of sirens on the east coast that had long ago agreed to refrain from eating humans and other beings.

Sirens could have called the Día Precioso to them. He looked around at the jagged rocks surrounding them. If the waters were shallower, there could have been a nest near the wreak.

"Fuck me, look." Hali waved him over and Tack saw a barnacle-encrusted lump. "Is this what I think it is?" she asked.

Tack studied the shape and gently smoothed a hand over it. "I think it's a Spanish swing gun. We'll have to uncover it to see for sure." He smiled. "This is promising. If this ship is the Día Precioso, we'll finally know what happened to it."

Hali smirked. "Plus, we'll potentially bring home treasure worth billions."

"Tack?" Harley tapped him on the shoulder and held out one of the bulky, underwater phones. "There's a call for you from the castle."

"Thanks." Tack stretched his back and put the phone to his ear. "Yeah?"

"Son," Nerio said, voice a little raspy. "We just received word that Prince Kit is pregnant. Your husband has begun packing and will leave Latch Bay in two weeks."

a wave of nausea caught Kit by surprise. He stopped trying to squeeze the suitcase shut and stood still, praying his stomach settled. He was a little over two months pregnant, and the nausea had been horrible. For some reason, though, being in the water helped.

"Daddy, is the baby grumpy again?" Pearl asked. His little girl was sitting in a pile of her stuffies, supposedly sorting them so they could be packed. Sorting looked quite a bit like playing to him.

"Yes, they are." He rubbed his stomach soothingly. "Carina, I'm going for a quick swim. My stomach is all messed up."

Carina looked up from the box of books she was packing and rolled her eyes. "Good. Leave the packing to us. It's kinda our job."

He shuffled his feet and looked around the half-packed room. "Are you sure? Those are my special books, and you can't mix the Italian BDSM romances with the Spanish Vampire romances."

Carina gave him a flat look. "The books are going into this box. You can organize them however you want when they get to Coalswell Tides."

Joy finished shutting the suitcase Kit had been struggling with. "Seriously, Kit. You leave tomorrow, and we can get this done faster without you here. That little bean has been bothering you a lot lately. Take Pearl for a swim at the reef."

Kit chewed on his lip. "You two won't mind?"

Carina rolled her eyes. "No, dang it. You, Dover, and Kai are the only royals I know that don't let the castle servants actually *serve*." She pointed at the door. "Go."

Kit snickered. "Yes, ma'am. Come on, Pearl. We've been dismissed."

Pearl jumped up, pigtails bouncing. "'Kay. Ms. Rina, be nice to my friends."

Carina laughed. "I'll treat your stuffies right, Pearl. They'll be all snuggly in their traveling homes when you get back."

Pearl grabbed the stuffed sea turtle Talia had given her a few months ago. "Tahli wants to stay with me."

Carina smiled softly. "Then we'll let her take a nap right here on your Daddy's bed while you have a swim. She'll be here when you get back."

Pearl hugged Carina's legs. "Thanks, Ms. Rina. Love you."

"Love you too, little bit." Sadness tinged Carina's

voice. Kit knew his friend really did love Pearl. Pearl and Kit would both miss Carina.

Kit took Pearl's hand and together they left his room. The royal wing of the upper castle was pure extravagant perfection from the expensive paintings hanging on the wall to the luxurious mosaic tiles imported from Versace.

Kit hated it. Cold perfection was hard to maintain and he'd given up a long time ago. He'd much rather be in Dover's cottage. He rubbed his thumb over the gold band on his finger. *I wonder if the iceberg of the north will be any better than here.*

"Daddy." Pearl tugged on his hand. "I have a question."

He smiled down at her. Just like him, Pearl had freckles across her nose and big green eyes. "What's your question, ma petite?"

"Auntie Lori said we was Coalswells now." Pearl gave him a worried look. "Are we?"

Kit rolled his eyes. "Aunt Lorelei doesn't know what she's talking about. You remember I got married to the Coalswell prince?"

Pearl nodded, grinning. "Uh huh. He gave you the pretty necklace, but he didn't stay to dance."

"No, he didn't." Kit sniffed, still a little annoyed about that. "The prince and his father had to leave right away to get home, so they didn't get to dance and eat cake with us."

Pearl gave a long, drawn out sigh. "Poor Coalswells."

Kit laughed. "Yes. Poor Coalswells. Anyway, since Prince Tack and I are married, we're going to live with them in Coalswell Tides. This means we'll be with the Coalswells, but we'll still be from the Southern Silver Isles, sweetie."

They reached one of the passages leading to the underwater portion of the castle, and Kit helped Pearl retie her sarong so it wouldn't get in the way of her tail before doing the same to his own.

They waded into the warm water, and Kit summoned his tail, then waited while Pearl did the same. He moaned as his stomach instantly settled. "Oh, thank the sea. That's better."

Pearl swam up and hugged him. "Poor Daddy."

He nodded. "Me and this grumpy baby feel better. Now, did I answer your question?"

Pearl pursed her lips and shook her head. "I got another. Is the prince my daddy now too? Affie has a mommy and a daddy, and Jill has a mommy and a mama. Do I get another daddy?"

Kit winced. "That's a hard one to answer. It depends on if Prince Tack wants to be your daddy."

Pearl blinked. "Why wouldn't he?"

"Exactly." Kit hugged her tight. "It's the best thing ever."

"Is it 'cause he can't kiss nobody?" Kit had already had many conversations about the curse with Pearl. She was a touchy-feely little girl, and he didn't want her to be hurt by an accidental touch.

Kit shook his head and pulled her with him as he swam down the busy corridor, trying to stay out of everyone's way. "I don't know him well enough to say what he wants, ma petite. You know he can't touch anyone, but he can still feel love."

Pearl nodded. "I can give him kisses anyway."

"No skin contact, baby girl."

She rolled her eyes. "I know. I got a kissy hanky."

He stopped swimming and gave her a puzzled look. "A kissy hanky?"

"Uh huh. I asked Ms. Rina to make it for me." Pearl pulled a white hanky out of the small pocket in her sarong. It floated out in the water, showing off the embroidered sea turtles and clownfish covering it.

"What's a kissy hanky?" he asked.

Pearl swam up and pressed the hanky to his cheek before leaning forward and giving him a big kiss through the cloth. "See? My kissy hanky. I can kiss anyone!"

Kit hugged his daughter, sniffling a little. "Pearl, you're so smart and loving. I'm proud of you, baby girl."

She giggled and pushed out of his arms. "Silly Daddy. Ms. Rina will make you one too."

"Yes, please."

Ervin swam past them, then circled back to them, wringing his hands. "Prince Kit. I just got the call. Dover is having the baby."

Kit grinned slowly. "Right now?"

"Yes. Dear gods, Shauna and Ben's hedge witch friend are there with him, but he needs one of the royal physicians." Ervin spun around. "I must tell the Kings and Queen."

Kit and Pearl watched the usually unflappable castle steward swim frantically toward the throne room. Kit gave Pearl a kiss. "Do you want to go see Uncle Ben? He's probably worried about Uncle Dover. It sounds like Ms. Hester is there too."

Pearl nodded. "I like Hester, and I can give Otis hugs."

"I'm sure that will help," Kit said, amused.

Kai whooped as he swam past, slowing down for them to catch up. "Did Ervin tell you?"

"We're on our way to Dover's cottage now." Kit shook his head. "Why didn't he come here to have the baby?"

Kai gave him a look. "He hates it here. You know that."

"Daddy doesn't like it either." Pearl grabbed Kai's shoulders and floated behind him as they swam. "Daddy likes Unki Dovi's house better."

Kai gave Kit a surprised look. "Really?"

Kit flushed. "You know I don't like all the drama here."

Kai winced. "We have plenty of that."

"Unki Dovi has better food too," Pearl added. "He lets Daddy eat all he wants."

Kai growled. "Did Mother put you on a diet again?"

Kit shrugged. "She just wants me to be healthy."

They swam away from the castle and toward the river. Two shark tailed Coalswell soldiers and two of the castle guards immediately moved to swim behind them. After the wedding, the four mers had been a constant presence when Kit or Pearl left the castle.

Kai pointedly ignored the Coalswells as they swam. "Did you check rotation yet, Harry?"

The sting ray tailed merman behind them laughed. "Yes, sir. Thanks for letting me off Friday. It's my anniversary, so my mate will appreciate it."

"You got her flowers, right?" Pearl asked, looking over her shoulder as she clung to Kai's back.

Harry and the other castle guard, Wally, laughed. "Yes, ma'am," Harry said, grinning. "I'm sure getting her flowers.

They talked for a while as they swam, but Kit started to tire quickly. Growing Tack's heir was hard work on his body.

Kit turned left and swam to a quiet spot on the river bottom, sighing when all of the others followed him. "I need a quick rest. You all go ahead."

Kai frowned. "Nope. No leaving the pregnant ones behind."

"We'll stay with him, Prince Kai," Wally said, nodding toward the other guards.

"Go." Kit waved his hands. "I just need to rest for a minute before swimming on."

Kai smiled reluctantly. "You're so bossy. You're going to make a good king one day."

Kit gasped and flipped his tail, smacking Kai in the butt. "Take that back!"

Kai chuckled and swam away with Pearl hanging onto him.

The four mers made a loose circle around Kit and he sighed. He had grown to know each of them, but it was still annoying to be constantly under guard.

Anabelle, one of the Coalswells, cleared her throat. "For the past two generations, the kings in the

Northern Silver Isles retire at sixty and their heirs take over. King Nerio is fifty-five."

Kit narrowed his eyes. "Ana, are you trying to tell me something?"

Wally chuckled. "I think she's pointing out that you *will* be a king one day, your highness."

Kit groaned and did a slow somersault. "Rude."

The other Coalswell, Luca, smiled. "It will be strange to have a ruling couple instead of one king. I think it's been seven generations since we've had a royal marriage."

"Why did Prince Tack change that?" The question left Kit's lips before he could stop it. He winced. "You two don't have to answer that."

Luca and Anabelle exchanged an uncomfortable look. "We don't really know, your highness," Anabelle answered. "When King Nerio announced the negotiations, we all assumed it was his idea."

Kit flushed, despite the coolness of the waters. "That would certainly make more sense." *Of course, it was the king's idea. Prince Tack didn't really want to marry me. Why did I think that?*

Wally snorted, his barracuda tail snapping beneath him. "I was one of the guards in the negotiations room. It wasn't King Nerio insisting on Prince Kit."

Luca smirked. "Interesting."

Kit fluttered his tail. "We've rested. Time to get moving."

Wally patted his broad shoulders. "Princess Pearl is a smart one, Prince Kit. Why don't you hang on and let me bring you there?"

Kit made a face, then grabbed Wally's shoulders as they began swimming. "I don't remember being this tired when I was pregnant with Pearl."

Harry swam beside them. "My wife says every pregnancy is different."

Luca and Anabelle swam behind them, eyes watching for danger. Kit rolled his eyes. The only places that were safer than the Isles River were the castle and royal beach.

By the time they reached Dover's waterfall, Kit wanted a nap. All four guards hovered around him as they walked down the cliff staircase and looked absurdly relieved when he made it to the bottom.

"I think we should call for a car when you get ready to go home," Anabelle said.

"Whatever." Kit scowled. "I've made this trip thousands of time. You all don't have to come."

"Yes, we do," Luca said. "Prince Tack would have our heads if something happened to you."

Harry nodded. "Since they're here, King Ren wants us here." He grinned at the Coalswells. "No offence."

Anabelle nudged Harry with her shoulder. "We see how it is."

Kit grinned as they teased one another. *It's been good having more than Coalswell diplomats here.*

"Daddy." Pearl ran from the front porch, Otis and another dog following behind her. "The baby's not here. Shawn and me are gonna swim with Mumu."

Dover and Ben's friend, Romeu, carried Shawn on his hip. "Is that okay with you? I thought I'd keep the little ones occupied while we waited."

Kit smiled. "Thank you, Mumu. You're the best."

Romeu gave Kit a flat look when Kit snickered at Pearl's name for him. "Why do I like you again?"

"Otis and JoJo can come too." Pearl danced in place. "So fun. I get you a shell, Luca."

Luca blinked in surprise. "Thank you, Princess Pearl."

Rachael eyed the guards from her normal perch on the porch rail.

"We're staying out here, right?" Anabelle asked.

"Hell yes, we are," Wally answered, glaring at the chicken. "That beast pecked me last time I tried to go inside."

Kit gave her a wide berth and headed for the door. "You four are such brave guards."

Nami and Eloise sat curled up together on a large chair near the window. Nami looked as if she were about to give birth herself, but she had another two months to go.

Kai sat on one of the comfortable loveseats. The scowl on his twin's face made Kit roll his eyes. "Why are you all scowly?" Kit asked, lightly kicking his brother's shin.

"I heard Dover yell." Kai's scowl deepened.

Kit groaned. "Oh, damn. I forgot how you were when Pearl was born. You get so angry."

"I don't like it when you all hurt, even Lorelei." Kai's scowl deepened. "I also don't like that you're leaving tomorrow."

Eloise gave him a nod. "Me and the rest of the

guppy tails did a thing for you. You'll see it tomorrow when you leave."

Kit grinned. "Thank you, Eloise. You all didn't have to do anything for me."

Nami snorted. "Trust me, you may not want to thank her when you see it."

Eloise gave her mate a hurt look. "How can you say that?"

"I've seen it." Nami rolled her eyes. "You're a bad influence on the guppy tails."

"Maybe you won't have to go," Kai said. "Maybe Prince Tack will change his mind about you going to Coalswell Tides."

Kit settled his head on Kai's shoulder. "I can't live in a different country from my husband."

"Maybe you can come home when the baby is born." A second later, Kai shook his head, grimacing. "What am I saying? You won't leave your child, and I can't hold that against you." He gave Kit a sad look. "The Coalswells are going to be your people now, aren't they?"

Kit was quiet for a moment. "I don't know. I guess that's up to them." He wasn't sure how the Coalswells would treat him and Pearl. Hell, he didn't really know how Tack would treat them. "Anabelle and Luca are nice."

"They're just two people." Kai squeezed his hand and leaned into Kit.

"Carina wouldn't say no to going with you." Nami gave Kit a soft look. "She loves you and Pearl, and that would give you an ally."

Kit shook his head. "I can't ask her to leave everyone she knows and loves."

Eloise snorted. "Carina is the feisty green-haired guppy tail that works in the castle, right?"

"Yep," Nami said, the word popping on her lips.

Eloise gave him a considering look. "Hmm."

Kit made a face at her, and she stuck her tongue out at him.

"Are you all really adults?" Kai asked, brow arched.

Before Kit could retaliate, their parents arrived. Kit hated the wiggle of jealousy at the sight of their joy and worry. When he'd had Pearl, Dover and Kai had been the only family members there. Dover had always had the love of the guppy tails, but now he also had their parents.

Don't be a douche canoe, Kit, he thought. Dover had put up with plenty of shit from the aristocratic merfolk in their father's court. Those same mers mostly ignored Kit's presence instead of actively bullying him or Pearl.

Ren sat down across from them and leaned forward, dangling his hands between his knees. "This is nerve-wracking. I almost prefer the muddled head I would get when something important was happening with you kids."

Kit eyed their father. "Huh?"

Ren flushed. "I think it was part of the curse. Anytime there was something going on with you kids, the plan was for me to keep my distance. I would start to wish I were with you, and my head would get all muddled so I couldn't think. I didn't worry about it since the plan was to remain indifferent so it would be easier when it came time for Talia to, you know."

"Kill you." Kai gave Ren a flat look. "That was the plan, right?"

Ren looked away. "Yes. I don't know why I thought it was a good idea."

Fergus and Kelby sat on either side of Ren. Kelby rubbed his back. "Fergus and I tried to talk him out of *the plan*, but he was so stubbornly focused on it. It was as if he thought that was the only way to truly spare you all the pain he felt when he had to protect the kingdom from, well, you know who."

"*His* father," Kit whispered, shivering. "Do you think it was the curse clouding your thinking then too?"

Ren looked tired. "I don't know, Kit. My plan doesn't make much sense to me now, but I truly thought it was the only way. When it came time for that final push to isolate you all, it felt as if my mind was swimming through sludge. I didn't want to hurt Dover or Ben, but everything in me said that was the only way."

"Then we wouldn't let you." Kai leaned back in his seat. "Talia and the rest of us said no, and Ben talked sense into you."

"It was still a struggle." Ren swallowed hard, eyes looking haunted. "It's one thing to know the curse exists, but another to feel it pushing you toward death."

"I could barely speak," Kit said, shivering. "If Ben wasn't there, I couldn't have stood with the others. All I wanted to do was hide in my room with Pearl and let it end."

Kai wrapped his arms around him. "All I wanted was to run Father through with my spear. I think each of us fought the curse that day."

"Mom said even the servants felt it pushing them." Nami's voice was almost too quiet to hear from across the room. "She said Ervin was desperate to rally the guppy tails because he felt something trying to push him to stand behind Talia."

Ren rubbed his face. "That damn man is a treasure. Seeing him stand *for* me and not against me was jarring."

"It's over now." Kelby forced a smile and waved her hands in front of her face as if she were shooing away a fly. "No more Sea Witch curse for the Rees family."

"Did someone say *Sea Witch*?" They all turned to the door and, sure enough, Sea Witch Johanna stood there. She wore a simple black sundress and her elaborate crown. Somehow, she managed to look just as regal as Queen Kelby in her full formal wear.

"What are you doing here?" Kelby asked, voice sharp.

She blew Kelby a kiss and sat down next to Kai. "Ben invited me, dear. I'm here to bless the baby once she's born."

"Bless?" Kelby arched a brow. "Are you sure you don't mean curse?"

Watching the two women was like watching a sparring match. Kit's eyes went from one woman to the other as they spoke.

"I don't do curses, dear," Johanna said, waving away

Kelby's sarcasm. "They're several generations out of fashion."

"If only they didn't last generations." Kelby huffed and crossed her legs.

"Oh, dear." Fergus's eyes filled with concerned. "The Muir family has its own curse, Kit. I didn't think about it effecting you."

Kit didn't appreciate everyone's stares. He flushed and sank back in the chair.

"How could it affect him?" Eloise asked, speaking up for the first time since the kings and queen arrived. "Wouldn't it only effect the Muir family and anyone who happened to be one of their mates."

Fergus looked relieved. "Good point."

"Well, witch? Can't you look in your scrying bowl and tell us if Kit will be safe from that horrid curse?" Kelby asked.

Johanna rolled her eyes. "I'm the Sea Witch, not a hedge witch. Ask Hester." She gave Kit a considering look. "What if you're a Muir mate?"

Kelby snorted. "I love my son, but there's no way the Goddess would match him with Prince Tack. The man is a cold-hearted and regal warrior while my Kit is an overexuberant, warm fluffball."

Kit laid his head back on Kai's shoulder. His mother meant well, but even her compliments hid insults.

Johanna twirled a strand of her long white hair around her finger. "No one knows the Goddess's mind. One curse is broken, but there are two more."

"Two?" Kai asked, head tilted in confusion.

Kit almost jumped out of his chair when Chubber

and his mother, Shell, ran through the open door and up the stairs. Their squeaks broke the tension, and he rubbed soothing circles over his belly.

"Do you think they'll try to help?" Kai asked, smiling after the two otters.

"Of course, they will," Kit answered, laughing. "Shell is Dover's other mama, and she's had three litters herself."

Kelby sniffed. "It's bad enough I have to compete with Shauna, but now I have to compete with an otter too. I'm a queen, damn it."

"It's not a competition, darling," Ren said, trying to hide a grin.

Nami laughed. "Mom said that since you partially have your head out of your ass now, she'll share Dover with you."

Kelby tried not to smile, but couldn't seem to help herself. "I wish I didn't like that woman so much."

A couple of hours later, Romeu and the kids were back from their swim, and the living room was full of guppy tails waiting for news. Kit again stifled the bit of jealousy worming through him. Dover had friends because he was a friendly, fun person. *If I had tried harder, I could have had friends too.*

They all tensed when they heard footsteps coming down the stairs. The grin Ben wore and the little bundle in his arms told them all they needed to know. They cheered and gave Dover's mate an expectant look.

"Meet our daughter, Prudence Rees." Ben's eyes watered. "We named her after my great-aunt. She was the only family I had that loved and accepted me. She would have liked meeting you all."

Kelby sniffled and hugged Shawn. The little boy sat in her lap, almost asleep. "That's a beautiful name. How's Dover?"

Ben grinned wider. "Sleeping now. Shauna and Hester are cleaning up and keeping an eye on him. He wanted me to introduce Prue to everyone."

Johanna wiped a tear from her eye. "Oh, Ben. Thank you for sharing her with us." She stood and moved to smile down at the bundle in his arms. She closed her eyes and touched the baby's forehead. "By the Godess and the sea, I bless you with a kind heart and a quick mind."

Ben hugged Johanna. "Thank you, Sea Witch. Start planning adventures for Shawn and Prue. I can see them exploring the isles with their friends."

Johanna laughed, wiping her eyes again. "I'll make a list."

Pearl bounced on Kit's lap. "I'll come too. I like babies. Shawn, you a big brother now."

Shawn yawned and snuggled against Kelby, completely unconcerned with the new baby.

Ben walked slowly and carefully knelt in front of Kit and Pearl. "Pearl, have a look at your new cousin."

Kit's lip trembled when he saw the red-faced, wrinkly baby with thick, blue hair. "She's beautiful."

"She's treasure," Ben whispered, face full of wonder.

CHAPTER 6

*T*he next morning, Kit's stomach gurgled. "Can't we just swim to Coalswell Tides?"

"It's too far." Kai gave him a sympathetic look. "King Nerio doesn't want our guards to go past his border, so at least flying is out."

Kit's stomach heaved at the thought of getting on a plane. "Thank the goddess."

Kai nudged him with his shoulder. "Cheer up. We're taking your new boat."

Eloise and Ben snickered.

Kit glared at Eloise. "I hate you."

Eloise gave him an exaggerated look of surprise. "What? After I led the project to make you this wonderful boat?"

The guppy tails of Latch Bay had actually built Kit a nice sized boat that he adored. They had some skilled shipbuilders, and this one was made for merfolk with an extra-long stern and nice swimming platform. He was truly touched that they had taken the time to do something like this for him. Then Eloise had to ruin it.

"You named it *TacKit*." Kit stomped his foot. "I've seen Ben's boat. You named it *BenDover*."

"It's your shipping name," Eloise said and started laughing. "Get it? Shipping name on your ship?"

Kai's eyes widened. "Oh, *BenDover* and *TacKit*."

"You're just now getting it?" Nami asked, rubbing her belly. "Good thing Talia is inheriting the throne."

Kai scowled for a minute then shrugged. "Yeah, you're probably right."

Eloise wheezed for air. "Shipping, ha!"

"Daddy, daddy, daddy!" Pearl ran to him, waving her stuffed turtle while Fergus chased after her. "Guess what?"

Kit smiled gently. "You've adopted a hippocampus?"

She giggled. "No, silly. They have to run free." She hugged his legs. "Ms. Rina says she's coming with us."

"What?" Kit looked around the dock. Sure enough, Carina was rolling a suitcase behind her and had her fat tabby cat tucked under one arm. Her parents and siblings surrounded her, all carrying more of her luggage.

Kai grinned. "Well, you will have an ally."

"He'll have more than one," Anabelle said softly from where she stood with Luca. "We'll take good care of your brother, Prince Kai."

Kai frowned. "You had better."

Luca fingered the shell necklace he wore. Pearl had made it for him last night. "Prince Kit and Princess Pearl will fit in well in Coalswell Tides."

"Yes, we will," Kit said, nodding firmly.

They all gave him surprised looks.

"Really?" Fergus asked. "Isn't the sea full of sharks up there?"

"Huh?" Pearl asked, eyes wide. "Sharkies not nice."

Kit glared at Fergus. "Grandpa didn't mean that, ma petite. I'm sure there are plenty of pretty places to swim with no sharks."

Luca coughed into his hand, and Anabelle looked away.

Great. We'll be surrounded by sharks. Kit narrowed his eyes. "Carina, you can't come with."

She gave him a stubborn look. "I didn't ask your permission. Prince Tack has already agreed that I can come. He even offered my family jobs if they wanted to move too."

"We're considering it," Carina's mother, Jaclyn, said. "I thought we'd let Rina go first and tell us if it's as horrible as they say."

"Is it bad, Daddy?" Pearl's lip trembled.

Kit glared at everyone. "No, it's not, baby girl. Remember, this is a fun adventure. We're going to learn all about the Coalswells and Prince Tack."

"We'll come visit, Pearl." Ben kneeled down and hugged her. "Remember what your Uncle Dover said this morning? As soon as Prue is ready to travel, we'll come to see you all in Coalswell Tides."

"He's right, sweetheart." Fergus leaned down and kissed Pearl's cheek. "You'll be able to show us all the best things about your new home, won't you?"

"Uh huh." She nodded and started bouncing again.

"Luca and Ana said they'll show me the best places to play, and Ana has a big girl just like me. She's gonna be my friend."

Ren and Kelby arrived with the rest of Kit's siblings a few moments later, and Kit took his time saying goodbye to each person. As annoying or indifferent as most of them were, they were still his family.

Fergus cupped his face and gently kissed his forehead. He kept his voice low. "Remember, son, a true treasure is far more than silver and gold. I saw the way Prince Tack watched you during your wedding. That man is more than he appears."

Kit swallowed hard. "He *appears* cold and distant. I want more than that. I deserve more than that."

"You do," Fergus agreed, eyes sad. "I wish we had been the parents you needed growing up. Despite the distance between us now, we'll be there for you."

Kit hugged him again, then let Fergus move away.

Ren took his place and hugged him tightly. "You are always welcome here, Kit. If they upset you in any way, just call. I'll come get you."

Kit squeezed his eyes shut, trying to memorize the feeling of his father's arms around him. This was perhaps the third hug the man had given him and it was magnificent. *Father hugs are the best.*

Kelby slipped in next, hugging him quickly before giving him a worried look. "I've sent King Nerio's cook a list of the foods you can eat. Don't forget your diet, Kit. You need to be both nutritious and weight conscious. You'll be king one day, son. Please try to curb your, uh, enthusiasm. Everything you say and do will be held against you."

He smiled shakily. "I'll do my best, Mother."

The rest of his goodbyes went quickly. Lorelei kissed his cheek. "Remember to avoid isolated towers and cellars. You don't want to find the crazy old king that they locked away. He'll probably eat your face."

"Love you too," Kit said dryly, rolling his eyes.

Once all the baggage was loaded, and their goodbyes were said, Kit and Pearl went aboard the *TacKit*, Carina following behind with her cat.

"Carina." Kit shook his head. "You really don't have to do this."

She shrugged one smoothly rounded shoulder. "I know."

"Can I play with the kitty?" Pearl asked.

Carina smiled gently. "Yes. Let's go below deck and get you and Puff settled."

Kit watched them go before turning back to the dock. Anabelle steered their boat into the bay, and several more boats pulled out and surrounded them. Kit new over fifty guards swam in between the boats as well.

"It will only take a few days to get to the border," Kai said, moving to stand beside him. "Then, Prince Tack will meet us and bring you the rest of the way."

Kit took his hand. "I'm glad I have a few more days with you."

"Me too," Kai said. "Hey, when your stomach gets too bad, we can swim a little too. Okay?"

"Perfect."

~

THEY WERE A FEW HOURS FROM THE BORDER WHEN THE attack came. Kai and Luca were taking a swim with Kit behind the boat while Anabelle and Carina watched over Pearl onboard. Latch Bay guards kept a protective circle around them.

Kit didn't know what was happening at first. Wally's startled expression caught his attention, then he saw the Latch Bay guard's blood filling the water around him and the harpoon jutting from his back.

"On the boat. Now." Kai pushed him toward Luca and drew his spear, eyes searching for danger.

Luca spun around, drawing his own weapon when a group of strange mers swam up from below. The looks on their faces made Kit swim toward the boat.

Luca and Kai tore into the strangers, but more appeared from below. In seconds the battle raged around him as the Latch Bay guards fought hard against their attackers.

Kit was almost to the boat when his eyes caught on Wally. The mer's barracuda tail twitched, letting Kit know he was alive but unconscious and bleeding. *I can't leave him behind.*

He swam as fast as he could, his short clownfish tail working double time to reach the guard. As soon as he did, he grabbed him under the arms and tugged him toward the boat.

They hadn't made much progress when three of the attackers began circling them, their shark tails cutting through the water much easier than Kit's. They held harpoon guns, rusty tridents, and long, hooked spears.

One of the mers smiled wide, his teeth sharp and gleaming. "Thanks for making this easier, princeling."

Kit glared at the man and drew Wally's dagger from the guard's side holster. "Fuck you."

The mer started laughing. "Aren't you a cute, little –"

His words were cut short when a great white shark swooped from below and bit him in half. The water turned red as the mer's lower half floated listlessly, the top caught in the shark's jaws as she thrashed her head.

A harpoon speared one of the others through the heart, and a familiar shark tailed merman cut the throat of the third attacker before the mer could get away.

Prince Tack's dark eyes glittered in the faint sunlight. "Get to the boat."

CHAPTER 7

*T*ack cut down another pirate while his mate clung to the bleeding guard. "Kit, you need to get to the boat."

"I can't leave him behind." Kit started swimming toward the boat, tugging the man with him. His clownfish tail was moving as fast as it could, but it wasn't fast enough.

Tack fired his harpoon gun and hit another attacker in the chest. Lola circled around and tore into two more. "Finch!"

The Kelpie appeared beside him a few moments later.

Tack nodded toward Kit and the guard.

Finch swam under the guard and lifted the mer onto his back.

"Kit, this is Finch. Let him take you back to the boat. My guards have secured it, so you'll be safe there."

Kit gave him a horrified look. "That's a Kelpie. They're… Tack, they're evil. They eat people."

Tack quickly dispatched a pirate. "Finch isn't too bad."

Finch whinnied and smacked Tack with his long tail of kelp.

"I promise you'll be okay. You can trust him." Tack gave his best reassuring smile but got the impression it may not have worked when Finch snorted at him.

Kit bit his lip and eyed the Kelpie's sunken dead eyes and razor-sharp fangs. "Okay. I'll trust you, but if he eats me, you get to be the one to tell Kai your monster friend ate me."

Finch kicked a pirate in the head and spun around to bite into his throat.

Kit squeaked and darted over, hugging Tack, careful to avoid touching his face or bare tail. "Damn it, trusting is hard. Be careful, and please look for Kai and Luca. They were fighting off a bunch of these mers."

Tack's brain wasn't working. Kit's arms were around his waist and he was pressed against him. *Bless the Goddess and the sea, this is the best moment of my life.*

Lola swam past him, nudging them with her side before she tore into another pirate.

Fuck, in the middle of a fight, Tack, he reminded himself. He gently moved Kit to Finch's back. His friend gave him an amused look, then kicked his webbed hooves, swimming quickly toward the boat and the safety of the guards.

Tack turned his attention to the fight. The Latch Bay guards were holding their own, but they were outnumbered. He swam through the battle, cutting down pirates and directing Lola to do as much damage as she could.

He spotted Kai a few moments later. He was back to back with Luca and surrounded by pirates. Luca's companion, a tiger shark, named Horus, swam for him. The shark had missed his friend while he was away.

Lola and Horus picked off the guards on one side while Tack helped Kai and Luca take out the others.

"Where's Kit?" Kai shoved the last pirate off his spear and pushed his body toward Lola. Tack's companion was quite happy to dispose of the body. *Waste not, want not.*

"At the boat. My guards have it secured." Tack looked around. "Looks like the fighting is mostly over."

"I'll look for wounded if you'll get back to Kit." Kai rolled his shoulders and neck. "Who the fuck were these people?"

Tack thought for a moment, then mentally shrugged. It would do no good to lie. "Pirates. They've plagued my kingdom for the past three years. They've been more active in the last few months."

"They wanted Prince Kit," Luca said, panting. He rubbed Horus's nose stroked down his side. "They went straight for his boat. The Latch Bay guards held them back. Barely."

"Ransom?" Kai asked, arching a brow.

Tack watched Lola weave in and out of the Latch Bay guards, pulling at the bodies of the pirates as she found them. For some reason, the guards were a little nervous.

He shook his head. "I don't know. They've never tried something like this before."

"They wouldn't like it if we were allies with the south," Luca said. "It would make things harder for them."

Kai sighed and rubbed his face. "I'll search for wounded and dead. We'll talk on the boat."

After he swam away, Tack and Luca headed for the boat. "Why is it named *TacKit*?" he asked.

Luca snickered. "I'll let your husband explain that." He watched Kai over his shoulder for a minute. "The prince is a good fighter. So are his guards."

"Surprised?"

"Yes. During the last war, my dad described Latch Bay as weak, but wealthy. They had more money to throw toward war, but lacked fighting skills."

"Not anymore," Tack nodded toward the dead pirates.

"No, not anymore."

They reached the boat, and Tack shifted, his tail slowly changing into legs. He pulled his black sarong down as far as it would go, hiding as much skin as he could before climbing onboard.

Kit was suddenly right there, hugging him again. Tack slowly wrapped his arms around the other man. It had been years since someone hugged him. *Fuck me, this is so damn good.*

"I'm glad you and Luca are safe. Is Kai okay?" Kit asked, looking up. His green eyes sparkled like sea glass. Tack could easily get lost in those eyes.

Finch grinned at him, phone held up and clearly

recording them. "Prince Tack? Are you going to answer the lovely omega hugging you?"

Tack scowled at his friend and tightened his arms around Kit. "Kai is okay. He's checking his guards over."

"Thank the Goddess." Kit pressed his face against the hardened black armor Tack wore. "They came out of nowhere."

"You're safe now." Tack swallowed hard. "I'm sorry this happened. I didn't think the pirates would ambush your people like this."

"Daddy, we can come out now?" A pudgy red-headed toddler poked her head through the door leading below deck.

A curvy, green-haired merwoman tugged Pearl back. "Sorry, Prince Kit. Anabelle said it was alright to come out."

"Toss me to the sharks, Rina," Anabelle mumbled, flushing when Tack gave her a hard look. "Finch said it was alright."

Finch grinned and nodded. "I did. The pirates are dead or gone."

"Daddy?"

Kit pushed away from Tack. "That was fast."

Tack glared at Finch. *A few more minutes would have been nice.*

"It's okay, Pearl. Come here, ma petite." Kit opened his arms, and the little girl ran to him. She wore a bright yellow sarong, and her dark red hair was arranged in two buns on top of her head. She clutched a stuffed sea turtle under her arm.

Pearl jumped into Kit's arms and hugged him tightly. "That was scary. Tahli cried."

"Tahli?" Finch asked, looking around. "Someone else on the ship?"

Pearl held up her turtle. "Tahli." Her eyes widened when she saw Tack. "Otter daddy!"

"Other, ma petite," Kit gently corrected her. "Not otter."

She reached into a pocket on her sarong and pulled out a hanky. "Gots my kissy hanky."

"Do you want to give him a kiss?" Kit asked, smiling.

Pearl nodded and puckered her lips.

Kit turned to Tack. "Lean down here, your highness."

Tack shook his head. "The curse –"

"Trust us," Kit said, eyes soft. "I trusted you, remember?"

He leaned down and almost jumped when Pearl pressed her handkerchief to his cheek. She gave the other side of the cloth a loud wet kiss, then leaned back. "Kissy hanky works good."

Finch made a gargled noise, the phone still recording.

Tack ignored him and rubbed his cheek, still warm from the cloth. "Thank you, Pearl."

She grinned. "Daddy has one too. He can kiss you later."

Finch squeaked. "Oh Goddess. Hali is going to be so mad she stayed at the excavation site."

Anabelle slapped the back of Finch's head. "Put that away and let's check on the wounded."

Kit nodded. "Your cousin Seamus stitched up Wally. He's the guard your friend helped me get to the boat. Seamus said Wally will be alright. He just lost a lot of blood."

"Good." Tack said. He saw his cousin cleaning the wounds of another Latch Bay guard and bandaging him up. The main deck was full of wounded, but at least they looked like they would live.

He looked at the waters around them. The other boats were taking on wounded, and the sharks were taking care of the dead pirates.

Tack finally started to relax a little. He had worried about meeting them within the border but had been too impatient to wait. *Thank the Goddess for impatience.* When he had seen Kit surrounded by pirates and blood, he had thought he'd go insane.

Kai pulled a wounded guard to the boat, and Tack leaned down to help him get the woman onboard. "We lost six guards and have a hell of a lot of wounded. Father will want to know about these pirates. They attacked our guards within our borders. That's not even considering they were after Kit. Talia is going to have kittens when she hears about this."

Kai carried the guard over to the main deck and set her down. He blew a long breath out and looked around. "It could have been worse."

Tack started to nod, then stopped, attention caught on his cousin. Seamus was frozen in place, eyes widened in horror as he looked at Kai.

Tack tilted his head, confused. Kai didn't look like he was dying or anything. The young man was simply catching his breath and surveying his surroundings.

"Otter daddy, hold me?" Pearl tapped his shoulder and held her arms out.

Tack blinked and picked her up carefully. "No skin."

"I know." She rolled her eyes. "I'm a big girl."

Tack hid a smile and held her on his hip. She wrapped her legs around his waist and settled her head on his chest.

Kai watched them sadly. "You'll be seeing a lot of visitors, Coalswell prince."

Tack nodded in understanding. He knew Kit wasn't happy in Latch Bay, but he also knew he had a family he cared for. A family that cared for him in return.

Kai stood. "We'll move the wounded to our ships and let you all get Kit and Pearl to safety." He smiled at Seamus. "Are you a healer?"

Seamus flushed. "Nope. I'm Tack's cousin. I just came along to meet Kit. Luckily I'm familiar enough with patching people up."

"Thank you for helping my people." Kai gave Seamus one more lingering look, then whistled for his guards. "Let's get our ships loaded with wounded and head to shore. Talia is sending reinforcements by air."

Kit tugged his brother into a hug, and Tack had to look away. He hated seeing Kit so sad. *Am I making the wrong choice? He isn't happy there, but maybe he could be if I left him alone.*

Pearl's breath tickled his chin. "Ana said her girl will

be my friend. I don't have no friends. Other mers are mean and call me names."

"Who calls you names?" Tack whispered, voice harsh. "I'll have Lola talk to them."

Pearl giggled. "Lola is a sharkey?"

"Yes. She's my companion, but she's dangerous."

"Like your skin?"

"Yes." Tack had spoken with Lola about Kit and Pearl, but a shark, no matter her connection to a mer, was still a shark. She was having a hard time understanding.

Kit sat down, face pale. "Donut sticks."

"What's wrong?" Tack shifted his hold on Pearl and crouched in front of Kit.

"Baby grumpy again?" Pearl asked.

"Yeah." Kit gave him an apologetic look. "I need to get back in the water. It settles my stomach."

Tack looked at the churning waters full of sharks then back at Kit's pale face. "Really?"

Worry crept into Kit's eyes. "Is it not safe? I know we'll pass by the Deep soon, and it would be better to be on the boat then."

Tack forced a smile. "Let's go for a quick swim."

"Me too?" Pearl asked, eyes hopeful.

"Why don't you come play with Puff?" Carina asked, holding her arms out. "Your daddies could use some alone time."

"Don't forget your kissy hanky, Daddy." Pearl used her hanky to kiss Tack's cheek again before he set her down. She ran to Kit. "You need mine?"

Kit grinned. "I have my own, thanks. Go play with Puff."

Pearl turned back to Tack. "I like kitties. We need a kitty."

Kit rolled his eyes. "Pearl –"

Tack snapped his fingers. "Finch, get a kitten."

Finch looked around. "For fuck's sake, where would I find one out here?"

Kai coughed into his fist. "Spoiled rotten."

Pearl giggled and hugged Kai's legs. "Silly Unki Kai. I really, really need a kitten. *I Need it.*"

Carina steered the little girl below deck, and Kai directed some of his guards in moving the wounded.

A tug on his arm drew Tack's attention. Kit's normal honey-gold skin was pallid. "Can we please swim now?"

"Yes." Tack pressed a gloved hand to the small of Kit's back and walked him to the swimming platform. "Finch, keep an eye out here. Anabelle and Luca, you two are with us in the water."

"Yes, sir." Luca jumped into the water, summoning his tail quickly. Anabelle followed him.

Tack helped Kit sit on the edge of the swimming platform before sliding into the water. He adjusted his black sarong and summoned his tail.

Kit slid ungracefully from the platform and into the water. "Is your tail cursed too?"

Tack followed Kit's eyes to his long, great white shark tail. "Yes. Lola bumped it once, and it hurt her. She's been careful of it ever since."

"I'm sorry, Tack. It can't be easy." Kit sank below the water, summoning his tail. "Oh, this is so much better."

Tack tried to keep his attention on their surroundings. "The water helps?"

"Yes." Kit patted his abdomen. "*Your* child likes the sea."

"My child." His hand hovered over Kit's soft belly. "May I?"

Kit smiled softly and took his hand, guiding it over his abdomen. "I'm fat, so it's hard to feel the baby right now. As time goes on, the baby will grow, and it'll become more noticeable."

Tack scowled. "You're not fat. You're soft and beautiful."

Kit's eyes widened. "Soft and beautiful?"

Tack spread his hands over Kit's stomach and around to his back, pulling his mate to him. "You're perfect."

Lola swam closer, circling them.

"That's a big shark," Kit said, hand gripping Tack's body armor. "She's what? Eighteen feet?"

"Twenty." Tack focused on his connection with Lola. *He's special, Lola.*

She sent him an image of a fat seal.

He groaned. *No, he's special.* He sent her an image of the birthing bay. It was a small beach on the east coast with warm, shallow waters. Lola always went there to give birth to her pups. It was a special place of safety. A sacred place.

He felt her understanding through their connection and sent her the image of Pearl too. *My pup.*

Tack froze in fear as Lola used her nose to force her way between Kit and Tack. *Lola, no!*

His companion ignored him and gently bumped Kit around until Tack's mate grabbed her dorsal fin. She took off through the waters, Kit hanging from her back.

Tack heard Kai yell from the surface. "What the fuck? Kit, get off that thing before it eats you."

Kit ignored him and laughed, hanging on tight to Tack's companion. "Lola, go faster."

"Well, would you look at that," Luca said, face impressed. "I thought for sure she was about to eat him."

Tack's fingers slowly loosened from around his harpoon gun. Lola had been with him since he was a child. When they met and bonded, she had just given birth to her first pups. The bond between a shark and one of his people was sacred, but Lola still had the instincts of a shark, no matter how smart and domesticated she was.

Lola swam past them again and Tack sighed happily at Kit's laughter. *Thank you, Lola.*

His shark sent him the image of the birthing bay again and he smiled. *Yes, he's my special one.*

CHAPTER 8

our days later, their party reached the edge
of Coalswell Tides. So far, all Kit had seen
of the Northern Silver Isles were rocky cliffs and two
distant coastal towns.

He had spent his time either on the boat or in the
water with Lola and Tack. Unfortunately, the closer
they traveled to Coalswell Tides, the colder the
water was.

His thicker merfolk skin could only take so much
from the cold sea, so now he wore one of the long-
sleeved black shirts that every Coalswell seemed to
wear. Even Pearl and Carina wore one. The special
design helped his body keep its warmth, but the color
made him sad.

Kit held onto Lola's dorsal fin with both hands as
they swam toward his new home. From the boat, the
city had appeared to be one long coastal town
stretching for miles down the rocky coast. Fishing
boats dotted the horizon, and a few larger ships could

be seen in the far away docks. The castle perched high above the town, nestled back against a thick forest.

It had been a serene and calm sight.

Beneath the water was a different story. The seabed along the coast was full of buildings made of stone and covered in colorful barnacles. Some were obviously guardtowers, but others were homes.

Further away from the coast, a long, exquisite cold-water coral reef stretched as far as Kit could see. Water sprites and a heard of hippocampi swam above the reef while merfolk enjoyed themselves below. The cold sea was full of life and color.

The surprisingly heavy traffic of merfolk caught him off guard. *Eugenia was wrong*, Kit thought when he saw the wide variety of tails. There were plenty of shark tailed merfolk, but there were also the ever-present guppy tailed mers, as well as seal tailed, orca tailed, dolphin tailed, porpoise tailed, and salmon tailed merfolk.

Several Kelpie and Nereids swam amongst the merfolk. Kit had never met a Nereid before, and Finch was the only Kelpie Kit knew. *Everyone looks happy*, he thought, shaking his head when he remembered his early worries about the north.

Apparently, even the Kelpie weren't so bad. Well, Finch seemed nice enough, and the Kelpie around them weren't eating anyone.

Lola pulled him ahead of the others, and Kit was reminded of one more distinct difference between the Northern and Southern Silver Isles. Here, sharks of every kind swam among the merfolk, as did several dolphins, orcas, and other sea creatures.

Tack swam faster, catching up to Kit and Lola. Pearl hung from his shoulders. She looked around in wonder, her round face full of curiosity.

A mako shark tailed guard swam past them, then zipped back to them, eyes darting from Pearl to Kit. "Oh shit! Prince Tack, you weren't supposed to arrive for two more hours. There was this whole welcome thing planned."

"We're a little early, Nolan." Tack nodded toward Lola and Kit. "These two kept swimming ahead."

"Otter Daddy, that's a reef!" Pearl pointed to the cold-water reef.

"Other, ma petite," Kit corrected, then yawned. He was getting a bit hungry. This baby loved the water and food with equal zest. He eyed a lobster crawling along the seabed. "Hmm, lobster."

"Are you hungry?" Tack asked, eyes instantly focused on him. Kit fought a blush. He had never had someone pay such close attention to him.

Nolan perked up. "I think the food is already being prepared. I'll call the castle and let them know you're here."

"They planned a welcome party?" Kit asked, a little disbelieving. "For Pearl and me?"

"You're my husband." Tack gave him an almost shy smile. "We all want you to be happy here."

"Can we play in the reef?" Pearl asked, patting Tack's shoulder.

Tack gave him a pleading look.

Kit snickered. "Okay, but only for half an hour. Otherwise, Lola and I are hunting lobsters."

"We need lobsters." Nolan abruptly turned away and swam toward the lower castle Kit could barely see.

Tack looked around. "Finch?"

Finch, in horse form, swam to them from the boat. Carina sat on his back, her green and black guppy tail hanging over one side of the Kelpie.

"Will you make sure everyone makes it to the castle? Pearl, Kit, and I are going to the reef for a moment."

Kit saw Finch nod his head before Kit and Lola swam past them, already heading toward the reef. Kit felt Tack's eyes follow him.

Over the past few days, Tack hadn't spoken a lot, but he'd been so attentive and caring toward both Kit and Pearl. Back in Latch Bay, Tack had been a stranger, and in most ways, he still was. Now, though, Kit could understand Fergus's words.

There's something hidden in my prince, Kit thought. *Something worth treasuring.*

"Daddy, look. She's pretty." Pearl and Tack swam past them, and Kit looked to where his daughter pointed.

A young Nereid woman swam close by, and Kit chuckled at her long-sleeved diving shirt. It had a large clam on it and said *Don't be so Shellfish*.

Unlike merfolk, Nereids didn't need time on land. Kit had the feeling the underwater homes belonged to the many Nereids he saw swimming along the reef.

The Nereid grinned and waved to Tack.

Kit frowned. *Why is she looking at my husband like that?*

She was beautiful with pale blue skin and long, tangled dark blue hair. Delicate fins lined her lower legs, helping to push her through the water.

"Grace." Tack nodded his head. "It's nice to see you."

"Prince Tack." She swam closer, long legs propelling her quickly.

Why is she only wearing bikini bottoms? It's too cold for that, Kit thought, scowling.

Tack pulled Pearl around his shoulders. "This is Pearl, my daughter. My husband, Kit, is with Lola."

Grace looked up and spotted him. "Whoa. I've never seen anyone but you so close to Lola."

Kit patted Lola's side and leaned in to whisper. "If she touches him, eat her."

Tack looked proud. "She enjoys his company. We're touring the reef if you and Jamie would like to join us."

That was when Kit noticed the little Nereid boy watching them shyly. He looked to be around the same age as Pearl. From what Kit understood, male Nereids were rare.

Grace smiled over her shoulder. "Well, Jamie, what do you think?"

Pearl pushed away from Tack and swam to the little boy. "Hi. I'm Pearl. I like your fins. They're pretty."

"I like your tail," Jamie whispered, blue cheeks flushing dark.

Pearl grinned. "Let's play."

Just like that, the two were swimming around Tack and Grace in a game of chase.

Kit knew he would be crying if he were above water. His daughter had always had a hard time making friends in the image-obsessed court back home.

Kit patted his shark again. "Damn it, Lola. I'm going to have to talk to the scantily clad woman with the nice ass. Whose ass is really that firm? Seriously."

He let go of Lola and slowly made his way to Tack and Grace. Kit maneuvered himself under Tack's arm and wrapped his arms around the large merman's waist. *Look at this snuggle, Grace. Look at it!*

Tack tightened his arm around Kit, and they slowly swam through the reef, keeping an eye on Pearl and Jamie as they moved.

"Grace works all over the kingdom with the hippocampi," Tack explained to Kit. "She's been out of town for a while."

Grace looped through the water in elegant spirals. "The herds are healthy and have almost doubled in size in the past five years. It was keeping me busy."

Kit felt a smidgeon of like for the woman, but he refused to smile at her.

"I've been missing so much time with Jamie, so I'm back in Coalswell Tides for good." She gave him a happy look. "You'll love it here, Kit. I know it's different than the Southern Silver Isles, but there is so much beauty around you."

Damn it, I like her. He reluctantly returned her smile. "It's not what I was expecting. That's for sure."

"When you get settled in, I'll show you and Pearl all the best swimming spots." Grace tapped his tail with

C.W. GRAY

one of her feet. "Jamie has had a hard time finding friends since we were always on the move, but look at him."

Pearl swam up behind the boy and tickled his side, before giggling and swimming away. Jamie laughed and chased after her.

Kit knew his expression was pure mushiness. "Pearl has a hard time too."

Tack scowled. "She'll have all the friends she could possibly want."

Kit snorted. "Are you going to snap your fingers and have Finch bring them for her?"

Tack shrugged. "That's the plan."

Grace rolled her eyes. "That's not how friends work."

Kit hid his smile. "He'll figure it out eventually, Grace."

His stomach rumbled, and Tack rubbed a gloved hand over it. "We need to get going. Grace, visit us at the castle when you can."

Grace grabbed Jamie as he swam past. "Will do. Come on, son. We need to go get some lunch."

Pearl's lip trembled. "You'll come with us? Daddy wants lobster. We'll share."

Jamie's eyes widened, and he gave his mother a pitiful look. "Please, Mama? I like Pearl."

Kit leaned over and gave Grace his own puppy dog eyes. "Please, Grace? I like you too. Not enough to share my lobster, but I can give you a roll or something."

The Nereid snorted with laughter and hugged her

son. "If it's alright with Prince Tack."

Tack nodded. "Of course."

Together, the five of them swam toward the lower castle. Pearl and Jamie held hands and settled their heads together so they could whisper to one another.

Kit looked around but didn't see his shark. "Where did Lola go?"

Tack tilted his head, eyes a little unfocused. "She's patrolling the black reefs. They're a few miles further out to sea. Many of our companion sharks spend time there when they want some privacy."

"The orcas go to the shoals," Grace said, pointing north. "The dolphins and harbor porpoises usually hang around here. They don't like being far from their merfolk."

"Companions." Kit rolled the word around. "Dover has Chubber, but I've never heard of merfolk having companions."

Grace scratched her ear. "It's not unique to the kingdom, but I've never seen it as widespread anywhere else, and I've been all over the world."

"My grandfather told me stories of our people learning how to bond with companions." Tack sounded thoughtful. "It only became common here a few generations ago."

Grandfather? Kit snuck a look at Tack's face. He didn't look too mournful or haunted. Maybe his insane grandfather was dead and not locked up somewhere. *I would at least look a little regretful if I had to lock a family member up. Well, except for Lorelei.*

Tack pulled them to a stop. "This is the lower castle.

77

Our steward is a merwoman named Petra. You'll meet her soon. She wrangles all the servants and groundskeepers." He smiled softly. "Truthfully, she keeps us all in order, myself included."

Kit's eyes widened as they slowly approached the lower castle. It was old, made of smooth stone and covered in dark corals and seashells. The high arches and sculpted spires somehow managed to be both intimidating and stunning.

The grounds around the castle were well maintained and clear of debris, but they were fairly bare. Kit was used to the seagrass and coral of the castle in Latch Bay, but he liked the simplicity of the sand and shells here.

Kit nibbled on his lip when he saw that lines of guards stood at the entrances. The pirate attack was still very fresh in his mind, and he had to admit he felt much safer with all the guards around. The slowly patrolling sharks also eased his mind.

Tack pointed to a large great white. "That's Dad's companion, Hugo. They don't get to go out much anymore, so he patrols the castle." He pointed at a Hammerhead. "That's Uncle Finbar's shark, Sara. She tends to stay around the castle too."

The guards saluted as they passed, and Tack nodded to them. His arm stayed around Kit's waist, steering him into the castle. "We have quarters here, but we typically eat, work, and sleep above. Will that be alright with you?"

Kit blinked. "You're asking my opinion?"

Tack looked confused. "Yes?"

It had been a long time since someone besides Dover and Kai had asked for Kit's preferences. He swallowed. "I'm good with that. Pearl and I both eat and sleep above too."

Tack nodded, falling silent again. Kit settled his head against Tack's chest and took in the wide, well-lit corridors. The floors were covered in a lovely array of dark sand and seashells while the walls were etched with carvings of the companions Kit had seen outside.

One caught his eye. It was a sleek sea lion wearing a crown. It stood out among the sharks, orcas, and dolphins. Kit snuggled tighter against Tack. *Backwards iceberg, my ass. Lorelei is going to be so jealous.*

Grace watched them with a smile, eyes full of something Kit couldn't discern. "What do you like to do for fun, Prince Kit?"

Kit blinked. His life consisted of taking care of Pearl and doing what he was told for as long as he could stand it. "Um, swimming?"

Grace tilted her head. "Swimming? You're a mer, swimming is a necessity, not a hobby. Anything else?"

"I like learning new languages," Kit admitted, biting his lip. "I'm not fluent or anything. It's just a hobby. Mother never thought it would be useful to pursue, so I haven't *formally* studied anything. Plus, I stick with the romance languages, and there are a lot of similarities between them."

"Daddy's really good," Pearl said, spinning around to swim backward. Jamie followed her lead and kept ahold of her hand. "He speaks fancy."

Tack let go of Kit so he could pull Pearl and Jamie

out of the way of a passing guppy tailed servant. He turned them back around so they could watch where they were going. "Be careful, little bit."

Pearl and Jamie leaned close together again, making Kit smile.

Tack pulled Kit back against his side. "Why would the queen not want you to study languages? Father made me learn a minimum of three beyond our own English and has always pushed me to learn more."

"Yeah." Grace gave him a puzzled look. "Wouldn't that be good for diplomatic relations?"

Kit snorted. "The last time they let me speak with a foreign ambassador, I tripped and pushed him into the laundry chute."

Tack gave him a considering look. "There've been a few people I've wanted to toss in the laundry chute myself."

Grace rolled her eyes. "Instead, you toss them to Lola."

Tack winced and gave Kit an innocent look. "That only happened once, and Lola didn't eat him."

Kit tapped his chin. "That's what *you* say. Anyway, Mother thought it was a waste of time." *Instead, she hired a nutritionist and personal trainer.*

Grace made a face, clearly not agreeing with Queen Kelby. "What are your favorite languages, your highness?"

"French and Italian." Kit also knew some Spanish, Portuguese, and Romanian.

"You call Pearl *ma petite.*" Tack's dark eyes glittered in the light of the lamps.

Kit had to swallow before he could speak again. *Has he always been so handsome?* Prince Tack's warm bronze skin practically glowed, and his short-cropped black hair begged for Kit's fingers.

"Kit?" Tack asked. "Are you alright?"

He cleared his throat. "Oh, yeah. Sorry. Um, so I guess studying languages is my hobby." *If only you knew what I liked to do with those languages.*

Grace shook her head. "Is there something new you wanted to try? Learning languages sounds like so much fun, *really*, but there has to be more."

"I see you speak fluent sarcasm," Kit said dryly, then thought for a moment. "I always wanted to learn how to cook like my brother Dover. Mother threw a fit when she found out the royal cook was giving me lessons, so I never learned much."

"Seamus loves cooking too," Tack said. "I know he would love to teach you."

"What else?" Grace asked, eyes narrowed. "You're hiding something."

He made a face. "Why are you so observant? Okay, so I like reading too, but not the proper stuff. Our tutors insisted on only literary works of fiction."

"Poopy books." Pearl looked back over her shoulder. "Daddy doesn't like them."

Kit laughed. "They aren't poopy books, Pearl, and I *do* like some of them. I just like my romance books more. I like reading them in one of the languages I'm studying."

Grace shook her head. "You've managed to make

romance books a learning activity. You and Tack really will get along."

"What's that mean?" Kit gave her a curious look.

"Supposedly he goes on all these exciting treasure hunts, but really he's just a staid archealogist." Grace sighed. "It's shameful."

Kit chuckled, and Tack cleared his throat. "Let's discuss your books. Not the poopy ones, of course."

"Daddy reads me good stories," Pearl told Jamie, "but Grandmama said I need more poopy books, so I get smarter."

"You're already the smartest three-year-old I know," Tack said, scowling. "We'll arrange for you to have the best tutors when you begin school, and I'll insure they don't make you only read poopy books."

Kit laughed. "They're *not* poopy books. Don't encourage her, tesoro mio."

Tack's face went slack. "What did you call me?"

Kit flushed. "Shi—shoot, did I say that aloud?"

Grace pressed her lips together while her eyes widened. She held her hands to her heart and looked like she was about to swoon.

No help for a distraction from her, Kit thought.

Tack pulled him to a stop and gripped Kit's chin in his hand. "You called me *my treasure.*"

"Blame Dover and Fergus." Kit wrinkled his nose. "They're always going on about treasure. I won't do it again. I promise."

Tack gave him a soft smile and let go of his chin. "I like it."

Kit's stomach growled again, reminding them all

that there was food waiting. Tack pulled him back against his side, and they swam toward a large staircase.

Nolan met them at the bottom. "Um, Prince Tack. Steward Petra said to, um, hurry up before she eats all the food."

"We had better hurry," Tack said wryly. "She's a merwoman of her word."

CHAPTER 9

$\mathcal{T}$he wide staircase led them above the water to a large, heated dressing room with several screens offering privacy. Two servants stood waiting to assist them, arms full of clothing.

Wind and rain beat at the window, making Kit happy they had arrived before the storm outside. It appeared that leaving the sea would be much more involved here in the north. He dried off behind a screen and quickly donned the clothes given to them – black slacks, a black button-down shirt, and a thick black wool sweater.

He glared at the black socks and loafers. "Why is everything black?"

He peeked around the other side of the screen and squeaked when he saw Tack's naked body. *My husband is fucking built.* Tack's broad shoulders and muscular arms led to a trim waist and a full, but firm ass. His long legs were as muscular as his arms.

Kit patted his soft belly and sighed. He truly pitied

Tack. If the man wasn't cursed, there was no way he would have chosen Kit as a husband. Instead, he'd probably be fucking his way through the gorgeous people that would have flocked around him.

Tack pulled his black pants up, covering Kit's new favorite sight, and looked over his shoulder. "The royal family, the guards, and our excavation teams all wear dark clothing. It's become habit, I think. Would you like something else?"

"This is okay." Kit said, forcing his eyes away from Tack's ass. "Do I need to wear the shoes?"

"The castle floors can be cold." Tack pulled on his shirt and dry body armor before pulling on his boots and gloves. He even had dry weapons to replace his underwater ones.

Kit narrowed his eyes. *Does he carry weapons and wear armor everywhere?*

"Daddy." Pearl stomped into his dressing space. "This is not okay." She pointed at her black dress, leggings, and sweater.

Tack rubbed his chin. "I can see the problem now. Black is a bit much, isn't it, little bit?"

"Yes." She crossed her arms, a grumpy look on her face. "I'll be good and wear it for you, otter daddy."

"Other, ma petite," Kit said absentmindedly. He stuffed his feet into the horrible socks and shoes, scowling the whole time. "Stupid shoes."

Grace and Jamie waited for them. The two Nereids were dressed in warm, borrowed clothing and looked entirely out of place. Kit had a feeling their visits above land would be short.

"Ready to eat, Jamie?" Kit asked, rubbing his belly. "I am."

Jamie smiled shyly and nodded.

Tack's warm hand on the small of Kit's back startled him. He moved to his new favorite spot, snuggled against Tack. It was different on dry land. Tack was much taller than Kit realized, and Kit barely reached his shoulder.

They walked the rest of the way up the long, winding staircase until they reached the upper castle. Muir castle was just as beautiful above ground as below. Rich tapestries covered the stone walls, mixed with family portraits here and there.

The halls were busy with black garbed servants, but each they passed gave him a friendly smile. *Okay, so far so good*, he thought.

"Tack, it's about damn time." A short, plump woman with dark brown hair and dark, liquid eyes stood in front of a wide archway, tapping her foot. "What took you so long?"

Tack winced. "Sorry, Petra. Kit, this is our castle steward. Remember that she's the one in charge here, and your life will be easier."

Petra's eyes softened and she smiled wide. "Prince Kit, we're so happy you're finally home. This big lug has been all out of sorts waiting for you and Princess Pearl."

Kit fluttered his eyes at Tack. "All out of sorts? Was the infamous brooding prince of the north *nervous*?"

"Did I say Petra was in charge?" Tack asked, rubbing

his chin. "I think I meant she was on her way to the dungeon."

She snorted. "Like there's room for me down there with your grandpa."

Tack shrugged. "You're right. What was I thinking?"

Kit felt his eyes widen, but he couldn't help it. *Lorelei was right about them locking up the old king.*

Petra knelt in front of Pearl and Jamie. "It's nice to see you again, Jamie. You, little lady, must be Pearl."

"That's me." Pearl grinned and curtsied clumsily. "Jamie is my friend. We're gonna meet Ana's girl too."

"That sounds like a lot of fun." Petra nodded and stood. "Beth is with her mom in the dining room. Let's go introduce you to her and get some food in your bellies."

Kit and Tack followed them into a large dining hall full of people. Several well-dressed merfolk gathered around King Nerio. Kit recognized the bored look on some of their faces. *Aristocrats.*

When he looked up, Kit gasped, eyes watering at the sight of a huge banner hanging on one of the walls with the words *Welcome Home* blazoned across it in bold lettering. Black and gold balloons floated along the ceiling.

King Nerio stepped forward. "Welcome to Coalswell Tides."

Pearl pulled out her handkerchief and ran to the king. "I have a kissy hanky. Daddy says I can give you kisses if you want, and Otter Daddy says I can call you Grampa."

Kit groaned and covered his face. "Shellfish and clams, Pearl. We just got here."

Nerio blinked, mouth opening and closing. The room of people watched him, faces varying from amusement to shock.

Pearl gave Nerio a disappointed look and her shoulders slumped. "You don't want kisses? Granddaddy, Grandpop, and Grandma like my kisses."

Nerio cleared his throat and knelt in front of her. "I would be grateful for your kisses, Pearl. Please be careful not to touch my skin. I wouldn't want you to be hurt."

Pearl danced in place, happy again. "I know. I'm a big girl." She pressed her hanky to his face and gave him a loud kiss. "Kisses for you, Grampa."

Nerio hugged her carefully. "Thank you, little one."

Another little girl wiggled with impatience as she waited beside Anabelle. Beth had her mother's caramel colored skin and dark eyes.

Nerio stood and waved Kit over. "I would like you all to meet Prince Kit and Princess Pearl. They've done us the honor of joining the Muir family."

Pearl tucked herself against Nerio's leg and gave the crowd a shy smile.

Kit forced himself to detach from Tack's side and went to stand next to Nerio at the table. "We're happy to be here."

"I'm sure you're hungry," Nerio said, waving toward the servants. "If you all will set the table, we'll eat lunch."

The servants moved to do his bidding. Kit tried to stay out of their way, but he stood right next to the table. With everyone's eyes on him, he was getting a bit nervous.

"Let me introduce you to everyone, Kit." Nerio turned him around. "You've met my nephew, Seamus."

Kit smiled at the younger man. He had traveled with them from the border, but Kit hadn't spent much time with him. He seemed a bit shy.

"It's nice to see you again, Seamus." Kit waved awkwardly, bumping into one of the servants leaning over the table with glasses and a pitcher of wine.

The young woman wobbled and quickly set the glasses down. Kit hurried to steady her, but moved too far, pushing her over in his haste. He watched in horror as she toppled over, and the pitcher of wine went sailing through the air.

It splattered all over one of the aristocrats – the grim faced, dark haired merman that stood next to Nerio.

The young woman winced at the mess. "I am so sorry—"

"It's my fault," Kit interrupted her, face red with embarrassment. "I'm too clumsy. I'm so sorry, sir."

Tack was immediately at his side, arm curling around Kit's waist. "It's okay, Kit. Uncle Fin doesn't mind."

Finbar wiped wine from his face. "Uncle Fin can speak for himself."

Petra snickered and patted the man's back. "You've never smelled better, Fin."

Kit wanted to sink into the ground. "I really am sorry."

Nerio waved his hand. "Don't worry about it, Kit. Personally, I think Fin's face looks better with wine on it. Let's sit down and enjoy lunch. I'll introduce you to my advisors here."

Tack pulled back a chair for him, so Kit sat down, surprised they weren't asking him to leave. Pearl patted his leg before she left him for a smaller table set up in front of one of the large windows in the dining room. His daughter was used to seeing him embarrass himself. Anabelle's daughter, Beth, and Jamie sat with Pearl, and the three leaned close to one another to speak.

Anabelle and Grace gave him sympathetic looks before sitting with the kids.

I want to sit at the kid table, he thought wistfully.

Once everyone was seated, Nerio got back to introductions. "Finbar, here, is my little brother. He's Seamus and Hali's father."

"Hali?" Kit asked.

"My daughter is leading an important excavation," Finbar said, expression somber. "Our best scout found a long missing Spanish Galleon from the seventeenth century."

Tack raised his brows. "They've confirmed it's the Día Precioso?"

"The beautiful day," Kit whispered, translating the name.

Finbar nodded. "They've made good progress since you left."

Nerio drew Kit's attention as he introduced the rest of people joining them for lunch. Kit tried to memorize their names. *At least they all have the same title*, he thought. Nerio called them all *Laird*, even the women. They all lived in Coalswell Tides and advised Nerio.

He was surprised that Petra was eating with them too. His parents would never have thought to ask their castle steward to join them for a meal. Each of the lairds, however, clearly respected the merwoman.

"You've met Finch already," Nerio nodded at the Kelpie. "He's in charge of the castle guard, but you'll find him with Tack most of the time. The two have been the best of friends since they were boys."

Kit noticed that one of the lairds seated next to Finch seemed uneasy. The man eyed the Kelpie as if he would attack at any moment.

"Laird Dougal, right?" Kit asked the man.

The man nodded and smiled nervously.

"Finch helped save a guard and me during the attack," Kit said, biting his lip. "To be honest, I've never heard good things about Kelpies, but he has proven to be a friend."

Finch gave him a bright smile. "Thanks, Kit. You'll get used to seeing Kelpie around Coalswell Tides. We aren't the murderous monsters now that we were in the past."

The laird next to him snorted.

Finch's smile turned predatory. "Well, not *too* murderous."

"Finch," Tack said, voice full of warning.

Finch sniffed and turned back to Kit. "Anyway, my

mom is Laird of Wynhaven Loch. A few generations ago, the Muir family accepted a herd of Kelpie into the kingdom on the condition that they behaved themselves. Now, most live here or back in Wynhaven."

The servant he pushed over earlier set a plate of tasty looking food in front of him with a wink. "Here you are, Prince Kit."

"Thanks." He smiled apologetically. "I really am sorry about earlier."

"I've spilled worse on poor Prince Finbar." She leaned close to him, so she wouldn't be overheard. "My name's Leona, by the way. Cook told me this wasn't part of your diet, but you was wanting lobster and that wasn't on the list your mother sent."

Kit shuddered. "I hate that list." The plate in front of him was a mixture of rice, vegetables, and skillet cooked lobster seasoned with butter and garlic. "This is so much better, Leona."

She patted his shoulder. "I'll let Cook know you like it." She refilled his water and went on to the next person.

Kit took his time savoring each bite of the deliciously tender lobster. "I preferred clams over lobster before I got pregnant." He made a face at Tack. "Your child loves lobster."

Tack looked ridiculously proud of that fact.

Nerio chuckled. "Already the proud papa."

The conversation stayed light as they ate, but once the wine was refreshed and the dishes taken away, the atmosphere grew subdued. Tack's warm arm stretched across the back of Kit's chair, so he leaned into his husband's side, yawning. *Yep. This really is my favorite place.*

"What are we going to do about the attack, King Nerio?" One of the lairds asked, drawing everyone's attention. "Ailig and his pirates have pulled the Southern Silver Isles into these skirmishes. I'm worried about how far they'll go."

"I'm working with King Ren to increase security along the border," Nerio said. "We'll keep looking for their base of operations. Meanwhile, I've already sent soldiers to reinforce each laird's lands."

Finbar's eyes grew sad as the others talked about the pirates. Kit thought it an odd reaction, but then again, he had never sat in on conversations about the defense of the kingdom, so maybe it was completely normal.

He settled his head on Tack's chest. All that swimming with Lola and his full belly threatened to lull him to sleep. *Time for a little nap.*

Finch leaned forward, eyes narrowed. "We need to find who Ailig is working wi—"

The door to the dining room banged open, making Kit jump. A white-haired merman in jeans and an old tattered sweat shirt came in. A slick brown sea lion followed behind, hind flippers pushing him forward.

"Damn it, Abernathy." Petra stood up. "I told you Earl can't come in the dining room."

The sea lion barked as he waddled past her and went straight to the kids' table.

Pearl and her new friends laughed, then set about

petting and hugging him. "Mr. Earl," Pearl said. "You are a pretty boy."

"Aw, untwist your fin, Petra. Earl is just saying hello." The old man grinned at the room and held up a small brown jug. "Is Kit here yet? I have a batch of whisky I want him to try. He's a new palette for me to play with."

Nerio groaned. "Dad, Kit's pregnant, remember? He can't have whisky."

Kit blinked and turned to Tack. "Dad? I thought King Nerio's father was locked up in the dungeon."

Tack gave a surprised laugh. "Goddess, sometimes I wish we could lock him in there."

Finbar gave him a puzzled look. "Why would you think –"

"My distillery is in the old dungeon," the old man interrupted, leaning over the back of Kit's chair. "We're all modern and shit now so we have a big ole prison inland, but the dungeon is reinforced and easy to guard." He leaned closer. "Bastards out there want my recipes, so they have spies everywhere. Abernathy Whisky is the best in the world, you know."

The man's words sunk in and Kit gasped. "You make Abernathy Whisky? I didn't know that came from the Northern Silver Isles."

The man's chest puffed up and he pointed at himself. "The one and only Abernathy right here, son."

Nerio sighed and propped his chin on his fist. "Kit, meet my father, Abernathy. He makes the whisky we export. We sell to one vender who distributes it around the world, so many don't realize it comes from here."

"It's one of our only exports," one of the lairds said, giving Abernathy a proud look. "It's made the kingdom a lot of money."

Kit laughed. "I can't wait to tell Kai. He loves Abernathy Honeybee Whisky. He's been drinking something made by the Coalswells all this time."

Tack's eyes danced with mischief. "Hmm, I think I'll send him a case."

"Come on, Kit." Abernathy pulled his chair back. "I'll show you my distillery since you can't taste my newest."

Finch held up his hand. "Wait, Aber. I can taste it for you."

Abernathy waved the Kelpie's words away. "You'll drink anything. You're a drink whore."

Finch gasped dramatically and pressed his hands his heart. "Don't drink-shame me, old man. Just because I like variety in my drink choices doesn't mean I can't appreciate a good jug of whisky."

Kit's chuckle turned into a yawn.

Tack stood up. "I'm sorry, Grandpa, but Kit needs some rest. We just arrived and he practically swam all the way from the border with Lola."

Abernathy patted Kit's back. "You get some rest, boy-o. I'll come get you tomorrow afternoon and show you the best part of this heaping pile of stones."

Kit shuffled from foot to foot. "I'd like that."

"Daddy, who's this?" Pearl appeared at his side. "Why's he wearing colors?"

Abernathy chuckled. "Not a fan of the black clothes, Pearl? I don't blame ya." He bent down, bracing his hands on his knees, so he could see her. "I'm your great-grandpa. You can call me Pappy, sundrop."

Pearl's eyes widened. "I don't have a great-grandpa. This nice." She pulled her hanky from her pocket and pressed it to his cheek. "Kissy time."

Abernathy grinned wide and held still as she gave him a kiss. "You're my favorite now, Pearl. I'll show you all my Whisky recipes and you can inherit the business."

Finbar rolled his eyes. "All your complaining about spies looking for your secrets and all it takes is a kiss to get them?"

Abernathy cackled. "Hell yeah. That was a good kiss."

Pearl went to the table. "You want kissy too?"

Finbar gave Pearl an affronted look, and Kit growled low in his throat, certain he was about to have to feed Tack's uncle to Lola.

Finbar leaned over in his chair. "What kind of question is that? Of course, I want one. You must watch my skin just like Nerio and Tack, princess."

Pearl giggled and gave the man a kiss. "I give everyone kisses."

A slow smile crept across Finbar's face and Kit hid his grin. *Poor Lola doesn't get a free lunch.*

CHAPTER 10

*J*ack felt surreal walking down the familiar hall leading to his rooms in the royal wing. He had an arm around his mate's waist and held Pearl's hand with his free one. *Goddess, is this real?*

"Here's the family library." Tack nodded at a door as they passed it. "You all are welcome to anything in it. We put up some shelves so you can store your own books too."

Kit stifled a yawn. "That's perfect. Pearl and I have a few we brought with us."

"Beth and Jamie come to play tomorrow." Pearl shook her butt in excitement. "I'll share my books and stuffies."

"That sounds fun, ma petite," Kit said, voice distracted. He seemed fascinated by the thick forest outside the windows they passed. Tack knew it was very different from the south, but he hoped Kit would get used to it.

Tack thought Kit's garden would help. "Once you've both taken a nap, I'll show you two something special."

Pearl squealed. "A surprise?"

Kit chuckled. "You don't have to spoil us, Tack."

"Of course, I do." He stopped at their door and nodded to the two guards standing on either side before opening it.

Pearl ran inside, head moving side to side as she tried to look at everything. Tack watched Kit closely. He had worked with Petra to make their rooms as comfortable as possible.

Kit's eyes traveled over the large windows overlooking the forest and the ocean, the television and the seating area, and the private kitchen and dining room.

"We get our own kitchen?" Kit asked, nose scrunched up in confusion.

Tack wished he could kiss the freckles covering Kit's nose and cheeks. He released a pent-up breath and crossed his arms. "Yes. That door leads to a bathroom, this one to our room, and that one goes to Pearl's room. There's more, but I'll give you a full tour after you rest. Finch told me your things are being unloaded now."

Kit gave him a funny look, then moved to Pearl. "It's time for a nap, ma petite. Today has been exciting, hasn't it?"

Pearl yawned as she shook her head. "I don't need a nap."

"Oh, but you do." Kit said, hands on her shoulders.

He steered her toward her door. "Let's see if your new bed is comfy."

Tack followed them into Pearl's room. He had insisted they repaint the room a soft yellow since that was Pearl's favorite color.

Pearl grinned and spun in circles. "My room pretty. Look, Daddy." She ran to the huge stuffed shark at the end of her bed and hugged it. "It's Lola."

Kit smiled softly. "Your bed is a sea turtle, ma petite."

Pearl let go of the shark and did a funny wiggling dance. "Like Tahli!"

"Oh, and look. You have your own shelves and I see a lot of new stuffie friends." Kit gave Tack a soft look. "Thank you for all of this. You didn't have to go to all this trouble, but I appreciate it."

Tack shrugged and grunted. He liked buying things for Pearl and Kit. He watched Kit settle Pearl down for a nap with her new giant shark, then followed him out of Pearl's room.

Kit yawned again, so Tack gently pushed him toward their room, his hand on the small of his mate's back. "You need a nap too."

Kit gave him a wry look. "Yes, I do, and I won't argue about it like Pearl. I wondered about our room. I wasn't sure you would want to share one with me since we won't be, uh, you know."

Unfortunately, Tack *did* know. He opened their door and led Kit inside. "I wanted us together. If you want your own space, I'll understand."

Kit's eyes widened when he saw the large glass art

piece hanging between the two beds. "Did Ben do that?"

Tack swallowed hard. "Yes. I commissioned him to make it to celebrate our wedding."

Tiny shards of glass built a swirling picture of the ocean. On the right side, the waters were a tropical blue while the waters on the left matched the dark blue of the Coalswell Sea. Each half had its own castle and reef as well, and tiny glass merfolk and sea creatures swam along the bottom. It was a perfect joining of their two homes.

"It's beautiful." Kit traced the light blue shards on the right before moving to trace the black coral reef on the left. A very small glass Lola patrolled them. "I'll miss my home, but your kingdom keeps surprising me with its beauty."

Tack's muscles relaxed at Kit's words.

Kit gave him a shy look before waving to the beds. "We can't share a bed?"

Tack flushed. "I'm afraid I'll hurt you while I sleep. All it takes is the barest accidental touch to cause pain."

Kit winced and nodded. "I understand."

Tack stared out the window. "I'm sorry that I can't be the husband you deserve. I swear, I will give you every bit of me that I can."

Kit was quiet for a moment and Tack began to worry. Maybe bringing Kit here hadn't been the right thing to do. Kit stroked a hand over the blanket on one of the beds before going to warm himself at the stone fireplace.

Finally, he came to stand in front of Tack and took

his hand. "Our home is lovely, tesoro mio, and our family will be too. Our marriage doesn't have to be like anyone else's. It just has to work for us." Kit tugged him to a loveseat next to the fireplace and they sat down. "I'm sure you heard about how Pearl was conceived."

"You enjoyed a heat swarm." Tack shrugged. "They're common here too. There are plenty of children born from one."

Kit snorted. "I wish my mother was as accepting as you. Before the heat swarm, she would arrange dates for me with men from the aristocratic families." He thought for a moment. "They were so cold. My brothers are better looking than me and Mother says I'm too *loud*. The dates were disasters."

Tack snarled before taking Kit's hand. "Obviously they were idiots." *Your mother included.*

Kit's smile lit up his face. "I'm glad you think so. Anyway, they were definitely not what I wanted or needed. The heat swarm gave me the opportunity to feel wanted – to feel beautiful – for a moment."

"I'm glad," Tack said, surprised that he truly was. He wanted Kit for his own in every way, but it hurt him to think of Kit being so lonely and unhappy.

"Mother was not." Kit looked away. "At least the dates stopped. She gave up on matching me to someone when she realized I was pregnant. The members of Father's court had never paid me much attention, but after that, they ignored me completely." Kit's laugh had a hard edge. "I tell myself it could have been worse. They treated Dover like a freak, but I was just invisible."

Tack shook his head. "It won't be like that here. I promise."

Kit's eyes softened. "I know. That's what I really wanted to say. I already feel more at home here after a few hours than I did for years back in Latch Bay. Your people are kind, and your family is *unique*."

"That's a good word for it," Tack said wryly.

Kit chuckled. "With a kingdom that bonds mostly with sharks, your grandfather's companion is a sea lion named Earl."

Tack nodded. "His first sea lion was named Billy. He fought beside Grandpa in the skirmishes over Brandywyne Trench. After Billy died of old age, he bonded with a sea lion named Joe. Now he has Earl."

"Aber seems like an interesting man." Kit smiled and stared at their joined hands. "He isn't the only interesting Muir around here, though."

~

WHILE PEARL AND KIT SLEPT, TACK AND CARINA directed the servants as they carried in boxes and suitcases.

Carina winced at the small box of books. "Kit will want to sort his books himself. He's only been able to sneak in a few, so these are his favorites."

Tack looked around. "Finch, we need more books. My husband gets all the books he wants."

His friend walked past him with a stack of boxes in his hand. "You do know I'm not your assistant. I'm in charge of castle security for fuck's sake."

Carina snorted. "Have you found that kitten yet?"

Finch looked down his nose. "I'm working on it. I'm meeting a guy at the docks in an hour. Where did you get Puff anyway? It's fucking hard to find a kitten in a kingdom of aquatic species. We don't have Goddess damned pet stores on every corner."

Tack shook his head in disappointment. "You're a horrible personal assistant."

Leona knocked on the open door. "Your Highness? Prince Seamus wanted to send up some snacks for Prince Kit and Princess Pearl."

Tack waved her in. Seamus was a trained chef and enjoyed helping the castle cook prepare their meals. Tack's cousin might not run the kitchen, but he spent most of his time there. Tack had never understood the allure of chopping vegetables.

Leona came in. "I think Cook and Prince Seamus have taken it as a challenge to find nice tasting alternatives to the list of foods Prince Kit's mother sent."

Tack frowned, brow furrowed. "What list?"

Leona set her tray on the kitchen counter and worked at putting the food containers away. "Cook said Queen Kelby sent her a list of foods Kit can eat on his diet."

"Diet?" Tack's eyes narrowed. According to Janine, his father's ambassador in Latch Bay, it was no secret that Queen Kelby often pushed her son to lose weight.

Leona shrugged. "She sent a list. Prince Seamus suggested throwing it away, but Cook thought Prince Kit might get mad if they did. That's all I know."

"Tell Esme to get rid of the list. Unless Kit specifically asks for only certain foods, he can have whatever the hell he wants."

Leona grinned. "That will make Prince Seamus and Cook both happy. Your cousin has been wanting to make him Lobster Thermidor since he's craving lobster, but that wasn't on *the list*."

Tack scowled. "Kit is perfect as he is. I understand eating healthy, but he should enjoy his meals."

Leona picked up her empty tray and winked. "I like those orders. We'll make sure Prince Kit eats well."

An hour later, Finch, Carina, and the servants were gone, and Tack sat on the couch, looking at the photos Hali had sent from the Día Precioso. They were very slowly uncovering the wreckage.

He heard the door open and looked up. Kit rubbed his eyes as he shuffled toward the kitchen. Tack's mate had changed into a bright yellow sarong and one of Tack's black t-shirts.

"Your feet will get cold." Tack set his iPad down and stood.

Kit's ass wiggled as he looked through the refrigerator. "Yum, lobster rolls."

Tack's eyes narrowed on the soft, round globes dancing beneath the thin material of Kit's sarong. He winced and adjusted himself before he moved to one of the stools along the bar separating the kitchen from the rest of the room.

"Did you bring any shoes with you? All of your suitcases are here."

Kit glared at him over his shoulder. "I hate shoes."

"The castle floors are cold stone."

Kit pulled out the container of lobster rolls and hopped up on the stool next to him. "You're a lot better looking when you don't talk about shoes."

Tack arched a brow. "You think I'm good looking?"

Kit took a bite of a roll and moaned, completely ignoring Tack's very important question. "This is delicious. I wish I could cook. I'd feed you so good."

Tack pulled his phone from his back pocket and texted Finch. "I'll eat anything you make me."

Kit set a roll in front of him. "Bon appétit."

"Thank you." Tack wasn't hungry since lunch hadn't been that long ago, but he couldn't turn away a gift from his mate.

"I'll go wake Pearl up." Kit took another bite and moaned again. "Are we still getting a surprise?"

Tack nodded and shifted in his seat again. Kit's moans should be illegal.

A little while later, second lunch was finished, and Pearl danced around the room. "I like 'prises."

Tack glared at the front door when he heard a knock. He couldn't wait to show Kit and Pearl the garden. He pulled it open and scowled at Finch when his friend pushed past him. He had a large crate in one hand and a tote bag in another.

Finch grinned and held up the items in his arms. "Uncle Finch has brought presents."

Pearl's eyes widened. "Presents is our 'prise?"

"No." Tack shoved Finch. "I'll show you the surprise *after* you see what Finch brought you."

"This day just gets better and better. Doesn't it, ma

petit?" Kit watched the crate curiously. "Please tell me that's not what I think it is."

Finch handed the bag to Kit. "For you, your highness."

Kit patted Finch's cheek. "You're so sweet, Finch. Thank you."

Tack glared at his friend. *Finch would look better without a face.*

Kit peeked in the bag and squealed. "I love them." He hugged Finch, then pulled a pair of lobster shaped house shoes from the bag. "These are perfect."

"I'm the one who texted him to get them," Tack grumbled.

Kit tore the tags off and put them on before hugging Tack. "Don't be jealous, tesoro mio. Finch can't help that he's a really good assistant."

Finch laughed. "Wait to say that until you see Pearl's gift."

Pearl smiled at him. "Present?"

He set the crate on the floor. "Here's your kitten, Pearl."

Her eyes widened and she squealed, sounding an awful lot like Kit. She sat on the floor in front of the crate and Tack heard a deep, rumbling meow. *That doesn't sound like a kitten.*

Finch smirked and opened the door. A very large Norwegian Forest Cat slowly stalked out of the crate. He went straight to Pearl and sat on her lap. It was a black and silver tabby, but the cat looked a little rough. One ear tip was gone, a scar crossed its nose, and its coat needed a good brushing.

Pearl's lip trembled and she hugged the cat. "My kitty is so pretty. I'll name you Chichi after Unki Finchichi."

Finch's smirk disappeared and Tack patted his back. "Isn't that sweet, Finchichi?"

Kit munched on another lobster roll and danced in place, admiring his lobster shoes. "That's the best cat I've ever seen, Finch. Thank you."

Tack blinked. He hadn't seen Kit go back to the kitchen for another roll.

Finch bowed low. "I live to serve, your highnesses."

Tack scowled. "My surprise is better."

Pearl looked doubtful. "Better than my Chichi?"

Kit chuckled. "I'm sure it is. Show us this surprise, tesoro mio."

Tack moved to the French door leading to Kit's garden. "If you'll follow me."

Pearl stood up, one hand buried in the fur on Chichi's back. The cat was damn big. "Come too, Chichi."

Tack opened the door and led them onto the balcony overlooking the garden. "Our seas get cold, especially in the winter, and they're much more dangerous than what you're used to. This is a safe place."

Kit's mouth fell open as he surveyed the tropical gardens, waterfall, and pool. He grabbed Tack's arm and tugged him over for a hug. "I can't believe you did this for us."

Tack let himself sink into Kit's arms. He knew his

expression was probably ridiculously blissful, but there was nothing better than one of Kit's hugs.

"Chichi wants to go swim." Pearl tugged on his leg. "I love your 'prise, Otter Daddy."

Finch picked her up and tossed her over his shoulder. "Let's go swim, princess. Your daddies will be right behind us."

Kit rubbed his face against Tack's chest. "Why would you do all of this for us, Tack? This is a lot of work to do for someone who isn't your mate."

Tack swallowed hard. He could tell Kit the truth – that Kit was his mate and he'd die for his love – but that hadn't worked out well for Finbar and Victoria. He didn't want to lose the tenuous relationship building between them.

"I want you to be happy," he finally said. It *was* the truth as well, just not all of it. "Let's go swim."

CHAPTER 11

A few days later, Kit sat on the edge of Abernathy's worktable and ate another bite of his lobster and avocado salad. The old castle's dungeon was surprisingly nice even though it lacked windows. The space had clearly been renovated for the comfort of a whisky obsessed old man and his sea lion.

Carina and Pearl played with Earl in his swimming pool on the other side of the massive windowless room. Abernathy's office was next to a small distillery. While the whisky was made in a much larger distillery inland, Tack's grandfather spent a lot of time experimenting on his own still.

"Now, smell this one." Abernathy held a tulip shaped glass under Kit's nose. "This is my newest blend. Strongly flavored and peaty, right?"

"Sure." Kit took another bite of his afternoon snack.

Abernathy looked around a moment, then leaned forward. "Now, don't tell anyone, but the two most important secrets about Abernathy Whisky is that we use the oils we get from the malted barley, and we have our own peat bog out near Wynhaven Loch. Finch's Ma keeps an eye on it for me."

Kit nodded, trying to look impressed. "Nice."

Abernathy patted his knee and went to put together another glass of grains. "I know you'll keep our secrets, boy-o. You and my little sundrop are part of the Muir family now."

Kit settled his hand on his slight baby bump and thought about the past week. "The Northern Silver Isles is a lot different than I thought it would be."

Abernathy cackled. "Did you think we were a hard and cold land led by an even colder king? Maybe you thought we were all monsters."

Kit flushed. "Maybe."

Abernathy's smiled faded. "It wasn't so long ago that you would have been right. My grandfather was a foul man, just like all the northern kings before him. Some were better at hiding it than others, but they were all selfish bastards that didn't care one bit about the kingdom or our people."

"They were that bad?" Kit asked, eyes widening slightly.

"They were." Abernathy sniffed the glass, then started adding more barley. "My grandfather was the one to offer a home to Finch's ancestral Kelpie herd and the colony of Sirens we have. It wasn't out of kindness neither. He wanted to use the Kelpie and the Sirens to take over all the Silver Isles."

Kit set his plate down, gut tightening. "I never heard about our people fighting Kelpie and Sirens."

"That's because his plan didn't work." Abernathy gave him a grim look. "He hoarded the kingdom's resources and practically starved his people. They were in no shape to fight. He sent his army to the Deep, and it was a massacre. The Kelpie and the Sirens were of no use against the Sea Witch. Grandfather died in the fighting, and we all breathed a sigh of relief when Da inherited the throne. He was a different man altogether and made it his priority to rebuild the kingdom."

Kit swung his legs as he thought of Abernathy and the other Muir men. *Tack will be a wonderful king and father, just like Nerio.* It still surprised Kit to see Nerio's genuine care and love for, not only Tack, but also Seamus and Pearl. He imagined the man treated Hali as his own when she was here. He hadn't met Tack's other cousin and had the impression it would be a while before she made it home.

Even Finbar kept track of his children and was clearly proud of each one. He bit his lip. *Father was cursed*, he reminded himself.

"Was your da a good father?" Kit asked.

Abernathy nodded. "He loved me and wasn't afraid to show it. Course he wasn't perfect. None of us are. We've had our skirmishes with the Deep and the Southern Silver Isles both. Hell, I started a foolish war against the Tuftfell Sea pirates, and those fuckers were a nasty bunch." He held the cup up to Kit's nose. "Smell this."

Kit sniffed at the glass. "It's lighter and more, um, grainy."

Abernathy gave him a pleased look. "Good nose.

This one is mixed with more grains." He set the cup down and leaned back against the table. "Da started the tradition of bonding with the sea. His companion was a great white shark named Delia. He wanted to strengthen our people by becoming closer to the sea."

"Bonding with the sea," Kit whispered. "I've never heard it called that. There are a few in Latch Bay that have companions, but it's not usual."

Abernathy leaned closer. "I suspect Da just really wanted a friend. The curse don't let us easily connect with people."

Kit twisted a bit of his sarong around his finger. "Tack has friends, though. So does Seamus."

The old man shrugged. "That's the young ones. In my time, folks were still wary of the Muir family's curse. My Grandfather heard the mating call and forced himself on the woman. He didn't want to wait, and he couldn't understand why his dick wouldn't make her love him."

Kit shuddered, completely horrified. "That's terrible."

Abernathy gave him a sad look. "It truly is. The poor woman died, and when Da heard his own mating call, he ignored it. It was tugging him to Morocco, but he didn't trust himself. He always worried he'd be just like Grandfather. It made for a lonely life, that's for sure. I think that's why Da turned to the sea."

Kit ignored the cold knot in his chest. He didn't want to think about the curse his child would have to live with. "What did he think of you bonding with a sea lion?"

Abernathy chuckled. "He was fucking scandalized. He envisioned his bloodline with shark companions all the way. Now Hali is bonded with an Orca and Seamus with a pair of Harbor Seals. I wish Da had lived to see it."

"Me too," Kit said, leaning over to hug the old man.

Abernathy stiffened before wrapping Kit in his arms and squeezing him tight. "You're good for the family, boy-o."

Satisfaction coursed through him at Abernathy's words. He loved his family, he really did, but they didn't need him. Dover had his own family now, and Kai was wrapped up in training the guard.

"Aber, have you heard the mating call?" Kit regretted the question as soon as it left his lips.

Abernathy leaned back but kept his arms around Kit. "Yes, I have. Every Muir will hear the call. That's part of the curse."

Kit scowled. *Tack better not hear the damn call.* Cursed or not, he was Kit's husband, and the more time Kit spent with him, the more possessive he was.

"What did you do about it?" he asked.

"Not a damn thing." Abernathy looked away for a moment. Vulnerability looked strange on the wiry old man. "You won't tell no one what I say, will ya?"

Kit shook his head. "Never. I can keep a confidence."

Abernathy leaned in close. "While it was hard keeping friends growing up, I did have one – a beta guppy tail named Cyreus. Nowadays, he's Laird of Riverpine Coast."

Kit thought over the names of the lairds he had met the day he arrived. "I haven't met him."

"He doesn't come to court often." Abernathy stared at his feet. "I figured out he was my mate when I was fifteen."

Kit rubbed Abernathy's thin arms and pulled him closer for another hug. "What happened?"

"I was too afraid to say anything. Every time I thought I had the courage, I'd lose my nerve. Then we grew up and he got married and had a passel of kids with his wife. He has sixteen grandkids and two great-grandkids." Abernathy rubbed his eyes. "I didn't have anything to offer him. The kingdom was only starting to recover, and this damn curse would have ruined our friendship. I live for our phone calls, Kit. I couldn't stand to lose him."

Kit let Abernathy pull away, but kept a hold of his gloved hands. "Aber, I'm so sorry."

The old man shrugged. "After Cy inherited his title and left Coalswell Tides, I found a surrogate and had Nerio, then Finbar. They're good boys, and I love them to bits. They've given me Tack, Hali, and Seamus. Now I have you and my sundrop. Family helps, boy-o."

Kit kissed Abernathy's knuckles, then let him go. "Tell me about Tack."

Abernathy chuckled. "He's a good one. Hali is as brash as can be, and Seamus is shy and sweet, but Tack is something else. He's smart as a whip and works hard for what he wants. Decided the kingdom needed to take more care treasure hunting, so he went to school and got a doctorate in archeology."

Kit smiled, delighted. "Really?"

"Yep. Then he trained his teams and sent them out." Abernathy leaned forward, eyes dancing. "He's a quiet one too. You'll never hear him coming until he's trapped ya."

Kit rolled his eyes. "He won't hurt me. Tack's one of the kindest people I know."

Abernathy snorted, then started laughing. "My grandson, Tack? That's the one you're talkin' about?"

Kit made a face. "Yes, that Tack. He's been nothing but kind to Pearl and me."

Abernathy clapped him on the back with a smile. "There's other reasons he'd wanna trap you."

"Why?" Kit asked, head tilted in curiosity.

Abernathy snorted. "Why, he asks."

Kit swung his legs as he considered Abernathy. "Are you trying to say Tack's attracted to me?"

"Yes, boy-o. That's exactly what I'm a sayin'." Abernathy muttered something under his breath and started putting together another cup of barley mixed with grains.

Kit picked at the heavy material of his orange sarong and swung his legs, thoughts turning to the way he felt pressed against Tack's side. "Hmm."

LATER THAT EVENING, KIT SWAM SLOWLY THROUGH THE shallows of his pool and watched Pearl giggle as she clung to Earl as they swam. They chased a sea turtle that looked remarkably similar to Pearl's stuffed turtle. "Come back, Tahli. I hug you."

Tack swam beside him, great white shark tail swishing slowly as he kept pace with Kit.

A few water sprites darted around him, smiling shyly before swimming toward the reef. Petra had told him that a family of water sprites made their home in the artificial waterfall.

Seamus and his two harbor seals, Betty and Veronica, darted through the reef, chasing the sprites and laughing. Carina swam up from the bottom of the reef and yelled, startling Seamus into laughter.

"I didn't expect this." Kit fought a wave of giddiness. "I didn't expect to like Coalswell Tides so much. I didn't expect to like *you* so much."

Tack gave him a soft smile. "I know what the Southern Silver Isles thinks of us. Sometimes they're right."

Kit nudged him with his shoulder. "Maybe if Nerio let Father send an ambassador, we wouldn't get it wrong so often."

Tack rubbed the back of his neck. "Dad remembers fighting with the Latch Bay merfolk. While he wants peace, it's hard to let go of the wariness and anger."

"I can understand that." Kit swam closer to Tack and waited for the man to raise his arm. He snuggled into his side, careful of Tack's bare tail.

"Your father has a hard time letting go of his own memories too." Tack's arm tightened. "I like Talia. She's good-tempered and smart. I even like Kai. He's done so much for the southern isles' defenses."

Kit forced a smile. "They like you too."

Tack's loud bark of laughter startled Seamus and his seals. They all looked over with eerily similar expressions.

Tack shook his head. "You don't have to lie, sweetling. I know they don't like me. One day, maybe I'll try to change that, but maybe not. As long as you like me, I'm happy."

Kit smiled to himself. *Sweetling.* He liked the endearment. "Well, Mother likes you more than she likes Sea Witch Johanna."

Tack's smile turned sour. "Lucky me."

They both surfaced when they heard voices at the door to the garden. Kit peeked above the water as an older woman with steel-grey hair and a plump figure walk toward the pool. She wore well-padded shoes and a simple black dress.

"Esme." Tack nodded and swam closer. "You got my message?"

The woman bowed slightly. "Yes, your highness." Her eyes caught on Kit and she smiled, eyes softening. "You want to learn to cook, Prince Kit?"

Kit popped his head out of the water. "Yes, yes, yes. Do you cook? What kind of cuisine do you specialize in? I have a recipe book in Italian that I'd love to try. Do you know Italian?"

Tack chuckled, and Esme looked at him in amazement. "Prince Tack?"

Geez, you'd think she never heard Tack laugh, Kit thought.

"Esme, this is my husband, Kit. Sweetling, this is the castle chef, Esme. Most of the servants call her Cook."

Esme eyed Kit, eyes full of curiosity. "It's a pleasure to meet you, Prince Kit. I like your eagerness. Mostly I cook the royal family's favorite dishes, but I have a fondness for French cuisine. My maman taught me everything she knew, so it brings back good memories."

"I love French food," Kit whispered, summoning his legs and running toward the woman. "Do you know French?"

She smiled gently. "Mais oui, bien sûr."

Kit barely restrained himself from hugging her. "I can translate the Italian recipe book for you and show you. You'll really teach me?"

Esme pulled him into a tight hug. "With pleasure, mon petit feu."

Kit flushed but didn't pull away. *Never say no to a hug.* His eyes met Tack's over Esme's shoulder. His husband looked pleased with himself.

Seamus waded out of the pool, looking excited. "I didn't even know you like to cook, Kit. Esme taught me, and I help her out all the time with meals. If you don't mind, I'll help teach you too."

Kit rushed to hug Seamus, careful of the man's bare skin. "That will be so much fun. Thank you, Seamus." He sent Esme a shy look. "I really can't wait, Esme. Are you sure it's not too much trouble?"

Esme rolled her eyes. "Are you kidding? I get another free pair of hands to help feed the castle. My budget has never looked better. How do you feel about starting now."

Kit gave Tack a questioning look. "Can I?"

Tack shooed him toward the door. "Go talk with Seamus and Esme. I'll keep an eye on Pearl."

CHAPTER 12

A month later, Kit snuggled under his covers, comforted in the soft snores from the bed next to him. It was time to get up, but he was so warm and cozy. *It'd be better with Tack's arms around me.*

He opened his eyes and watched the early sunshine fall across his husband's sharp featured face. After his talk with Abernathy, Kit had noticed that Tack was a ball of contradictions stuffed into a gorgeous package. With Pearl and Kit, Tack was the sweetest man alive. He was patient, giving, and kind.

With others, he was still kind, but also quiet and a little stern. He seldom smiled, but damn, when he did, it was a beautiful thing.

Kit wished he could kiss Tack's soft looking lips. *There has to be a way.*

Tack's eyes fluttered open right before the alarm went off. A sleepy smile crept across his face, and Kit grinned back at him. "I'm surprised our little bit hasn't —"

The door banged open, and Pearl and Chichi ran inside. "Daddies. Chichi and me are hungry. We need brekkie and want to eat with Grampa."

Kit smiled. "Okay, ma petit. We'll get up."

Pearl jumped onto his bed and snuggled up against him, pressing her ear to his belly. "Sing the baby song?"

Kit chuckled. "Go ahead."

"Baby come swim with Chichi and me," Pearl sang off key. "We swim with Lola, Beth, and Jamie under the sea."

Kit waited for Pearl to finish singing her song, then sat up. "I bet the baby liked that."

Pearl giggled and hopped off the bed. "Hurry! I'm hungry." She ran out the door, Chichi following behind her.

Kit tossed a pillow at Tack. The man was watching him with one of his shivery smiles. "Do you think the doctor will be able to tell us the gender today?"

"I hope so." Tack got out of bed and stretched his arms over his head. "Dad and Grandpa have been bugging the shit out of me about it."

Kit forced himself to look away from Tack and pick out clothes for the day. "Okay, so the doctor's appointment is after lunch. Are you hanging out with Pearl and me today?"

"If you don't mind." Tack grinned over his shoulder. "I have some work to do this afternoon, but I thought we'd take a swim after breakfast."

"Perfect." Kit grabbed his phone and sent a text to Kai, asking him to call after lunch. He needed some advice. "I have a lesson with Esme today at two. We're making honey glazed salmon for dinner."

"Hmm, that sounds good." Tack pulled on his usual, black armored clothing and boots while Kit knotted his favorite orange sarong around his hips and pulled on his new bright blue wool kimono.

He slipped into his lobster shoes and went to wrangle Pearl into her clothes.

By the time they reached the smaller dining room in the royal wing, Kit was starving. He was right at four months pregnant and while the nausea was gone, the hunger had only increased.

Nerio and the others were already there when they arrived. Kit hummed happily when he saw their plates piled high with food. *Esme is so good to me.*

Pearl ran straight to Seamus and climbed into the omega's lap while Tack helped Kit sit. "Unki Shay, I'll give you kisses."

Kit focused on the porridge and eggs in front of him. Esme had topped the porridge with bananas and granola. *Just how I like it.*

"Today's the big day, right?" Nerio asked, leaning forward. "The doctor said he could tell us the gender at four months."

"He said he *might* be able to tell us the gender." Petra refilled Nerio's coffee cup, then sat at her own seat. Kit had found it strange that Petra ate with the family, but he adored her, so he didn't question it.

Abernathy tossed a sardine to Earl. "Gender don't matter. As long as the baby is healthy, we'll be happy."

Petra narrowed her eyes. "When I was pregnant

with the twins, you sure were worried about me having a boy."

Kit looked up from his eggs. "You have children? Do they live around here?"

Everyone at the table stared at him in silence.

Kit blinked. "What?"

Finbar arched a brow. "Petra was my surrogate for Hali and Seamus. She's their mother."

Kit frowned. "I've been here a month. How did I not know this?"

Pearl finishing chewing a bite of her toast. "Everybody knows it, Daddy."

Kit's shoulders slumped. "I thought she was just the castle steward."

Petra looked confused. "Does the castle steward eat with your family in Latch Bay?"

"Well, no, but you run everything. I figured you were letting *us* eat with *you.*"

Petra walked around the table and hugged him. "I do love you, Kit. I'll let you eat meals with me anytime."

"Thank you." Kit ate some of his porridge and ignored the laughter around him.

Finch pointed his fork at Kit. "Just so you know, I'm not related. I just like free food, and they haven't kicked me out yet."

"Yet," Tack said slowly, drawing the word out. "Chichi puked in my boots yesterday."

"Chichi said she sorry." Pearl gave Tack a sad look. "You forgive him, right?"

Tack crumbled. "Of course, baby girl."

Nerio smiled and sipped his coffee. "Tack's

surrogate was a lovely omega from the east coast. His father is one of my most trusted advisors."

Kit nudged Tack with his shoulder. "You have another dad?"

"Not really." Tack shrugged. "Neyland was just Dad's surrogate. He went on to marry and have his own family after I was born. We see one another occasionally, but it's not like Petra and the twins."

Nerio winced. "If I would have thought of asking Petra to be my surrogate, I would have. She's an excellent mother."

Petra glowed at the praise. "I am." She aimed a hard stare at Tack. "You're mine too, Tack. I may not have birthed you, but I sure changed enough of your diapers to be your mama."

Kit smiled again. *Yep, I like the woman.*

AFTER A LONG AND RELAXING SWIM IN HIS POOL, KIT LAY back in his bed and let Dr. Giles roll the transducer probe over his abdomen. Tack's family stood around the bed, watching closely, while Tack sat beside Kit on the bed, holding his hand.

The doctor watched the monitor of the portable ultrasound with a smile. "The heartbeat is strong, and the baby isn't very modest. You're having a boy."

Nerio whooped and bounced Pearl on his hip. "You're gonna have a brother, little one."

Abernathy hugged Earl. "Kit, you should name him Abernathy the second."

Earl barked excitedly and waddled closer to Kit's bed.

"For the love of pickled herring, what is that sea lion doing in Tack and Kit's room?" Petra glared at Abernathy. "I told you to keep him in the halls only, Aber."

Kit giggled. He loved watching Petra and Aber argue over Earl.

"Congratulations." Finbar gave Kit a soft look and pulled a stuffed clownfish from behind him. "For the baby."

Kit gave the man a nervous smile and took the stuffie. Over the past month, Finbar had remained friendly but distant. "Thank... Oh, fuck. I still have to put together the nursery."

Tack patted his hand. "We have plenty of time. I'll have Finch start making a list."

Finbar arched a brow. "You do know Finch is the commander of the castle guard, correct?"

Tack crossed his arms and smirked. "Your point would be?"

The doctor shook his head and packed up his tools. "I'll see you for a full exam in another week, Prince Kit. Get plenty of exercise, but rest when you need to. Eat plenty of dairy, leafy greens, and salmon."

"Yes, sir." Kit yawned. "Lobster is okay, right?"

The doctor smiled and patted his shoulder. "Yes, but go light on the butter."

"Butter makes everything better," he whispered, eyes watering. *Stupid emotions are all over the place lately.*

Tack smoothed a gloved hand through Kit's hair.

"I'll get these weirdos out of here and put Pearl down for her nap. Lay down and rest, alright?"

Kit nodded and hugged the stuffed clownfish. "Good idea."

He watched Tack herd his family out of the bedroom, then settled back on the bed and stared at the ceiling for a moment before he sat up and grabbed his phone from the bedtable. He carried the clownfish stuffie to his favorite napping spot – a plush window seat overlooking the forest and ocean. Carina had left his favorite blanket folded up on the back of it, right beside one of his new books. Finch had brought him a box of gay romances in Italian, Spanish, and French. *Such a good personal assistant.*

He pressed his face against the glass and watched the trees sway in the breeze. Fairy lights flickered here and there within the trees, and Kit smiled. He hadn't managed to make it into the woods yet. He was too enamored with his garden. He had made time to swim with Lola and explore the reefs with Grace, but the woods were calling to him. *Maybe tomorrow.*

His phone rang and he answered it without looking at the number. "Kai, I have a problem."

"Who do I need to kill? Are you and Pearl coming home? Wait, I'll grab Talia, and we'll round up some guards." It was good to hear his brother's voice even if Kai was being ridiculous.

"No, I love it here with Tack and his family." Kit watched as a tiny fairy flew up above the trees. "That's the problem. I really want my marriage to work. Tack is a good man, Kai."

"Prince Tack? The silent, cold-hearted bastard of the north?"

Kit rolled his eyes. "He's not a cold-hearted bastard, and he's only silent around people he doesn't like."

"Like me?"

"Did you get the case of whisky?" Kit waved at the fairy as she flew close to his window. He could see her wild brown hair and dirt-covered leaf dress.

"I burned his note. I'm pretending I never read it, so I don't know where my whisky comes from." Kit growled. "Okay, so you're happy. What's the problem?"

"I want to be with him." Kit cracked his window, and the fairy peeked inside, looking around.

"Be with him? Aren't you living with the man?"

Kit chewed on his lip. "Tack is such a good person, Kai. He is always doing small things to make Pearl and me happy, and he spends so much time with us. I didn't expect him to snuggle with me in the evenings to watch television or have tea parties with Pearl and Chichi. Kai, he even buys me romance books and lets me test my cooking skills on him."

"You're talking about Prince Tack?"

"Yes." Kit sighed, frustrated. "I know sex is just one way to connect with someone, but the more I'm around Tack, the more I want to have a physical relationship with him. I know I'm not the most attractive person in the world, but I think we could enjoy each other."

Kai groaned. "Goddess help me. I want to bleach my brain at the image of you two fucking, but I also want to tell you that you're beautiful and that damned Coalswell would be lucky to get to fuck you."

Kit giggled and held his hand out to the fairy. She watched him suspiciously for a moment, then balanced on his palm. He had never been so close to a fairy before.

She knelt and sniffed his hand, then gently nibbled on his thumb. She made a face at the taste and stuck her tongue out at him before flitting away to search the room.

"Ma petite fée," he whispered. "Hey, what do fairies eat?"

"Thank you, Goddess, for the topic change," Kai said. "Fairies love sugar, but in the wild they eat acorns, leaves, pollen, and flower petals."

"Not people?"

"What kind of fairies do they have in the north?" Kai asked, voice rising. "Cannibal fairies?"

"Just making sure. Now, about sex with Tack. I need help figuring out what to do. We can't touch skin to skin, but there has to be another way, right?"

Kai groaned. "Call Dover."

Kit heard the call end and stared at the phone. "The fucker hung up on me."

The fairy flew over and glared at the phone before smacking it.

"I know, right?" Kit scowled. "I guess I'll try Dover."

He pressed his brother's name and waited for him to pick up. "Kit? Did the sharks eat Pearl? Do we need to come get you?"

Kit groaned. "Pearl and I are fine. I need sex advice."

"You can't cheat on Prince Tack. That would just be cruel."

"I would never cheat on someone," Kit said, scowling. "I want to have sex with Tack."

"Well, you can't. His dick will kill you."

Kit buried his face against a pillow and screamed. He felt the fairy pat his head.

He leaned back up and put the phone to his ear again. "I'm aware we can't touch. I need ideas to get around that."

"I don't want you to die." Dover sniffled. "Just watch porn and masturbate. It's the safe thing to do."

"Dover," he growled.

"Shawn and Prue are doing well." Dover ignored him. "Shawn is fully potty trained now. Isn't that great? He's so smart. Oh, and Prue smiles at me all the time. She's going to be a happy baby."

"She's probably just farting."

"Clearly, you're in no mood to talk." Dover tsked. "I'll call you tonight so you can apologize."

Kit glared at the phone as the call ended. "He hung up on me too, fairy. What the hell?"

The fairy shrugged.

Kit closed his eyes. He knew Dover would call him later and apologize for snapping at him, but he needed answers now. "There's one more person to try, but I *really* don't want to do this."

The fairy propped her hands on her hips and gave him a hard look.

"You're right. I have to do it." He dialed her number.

Lorelei answered right away. "Please tell me Prince

Tack has decided to feed you to his crazy grandfather and marry me. Don't worry. I'll take good care of Pearl."

"I hate you."

"Then why did you call?"

He made a face. "I need some advice."

"Lose forty pounds, dye your hair blond, and work out. Your musculature is pitiful. Then you should update your wardrobe and stop wearing orange and yellow. Try dark green instead."

His teeth ground together, but he managed not to smash his phone against the window. The fairy flew to the top of his head and hugged him, her tiny squeaks strangely soothing.

"I mean, I need sex advice," he finally ground out.

"Oh, Kit," Lorelei practically purred. "I thought you'd never ask."

CHAPTER 13

*A*few days later, Kit smiled nervously at the two guards at his door as he let Petra and Carina into his rooms. *Nothing to see here. They aren't carrying a box of sex toys.*

As soon as the door was shut, he leaned back against it and took a calming breath. "Did you bring the stuff?"

Carina held up the box she carried. "What does this look like to you?"

"A box."

Petra gave him an understanding look. "You don't have to be nervous."

Tack and Pearl were visiting with Lola, so at least he didn't have to do this with them right there.

Kit followed the women to his bedroom, trying to peek over Carina's shoulder at the contents of the box. "What if he thinks I'm weird?"

Carina set the box on his bed, then pushed him away before she started unpacking it.

Petra pulled him to her and patted his cheek. "We all already know you're weird, sweetheart. That's why you fit in so well." She gestured to the box. "This, though, isn't weird; it's extremely sweet. I can't believe no one has tried this before. Well, that I know of anyway."

"It's odd that they haven't." Carina pushed him away again. "I can't imagine going without sex."

"Sex is just one way of being intimate." Kit shoved past her and pulled long velvet gloves from the box. "Going without touch entirely, though. That has to be hard."

An agonized look flashed across Petra's face. "I hated not being able to touch my Hali and Seamus. Cuddling them through a blanket wasn't enough. I remember Seamus reaching for me when he was a baby before he knew better. I couldn't resist letting his little hand hold my finger."

Kit cupped his stomach protectively. "What happened?"

"I passed out from the pain." Petra wiped at her tears. "I woke up to him crying. He didn't know what happened."

"I didn't think about never touching my son." Kit's hand trembled against his abdomen. "The curse takes effect right away?"

"Thirty minutes after they're born." Petra unpacked the box, laying each item on his bed. "I had thirty minutes to kiss and hold my babies before the damned curse took that from me."

"Who held Tack?" Kit thought about Tack's

surrogate. It hadn't sounded like he was that close to the omega.

"His nanny, Tilda." Petra pushed her hair from her eyes. "Neyland never saw Tack as a *son*. To him, carrying the king's heir was an honor, but also merely a service to be completed. Tilda loved Tack as her own. It broke our hearts when she passed away."

"One of my earliest memories is of Mother rocking me in her lap and singing a lullaby. I remember Fergus standing behind us, singing along. As much of a pain as she is, she's always been there."

They all looked toward the window when they heard tiny pings against the glass.

"Is that a fairy knocking on your window?" Carina asked, surprised.

"Yeah, I gave her some sugar yesterday, so she's probably here for more." Kit went to let the fairy in.

She flew in circles around his head before going to the dresser. He had wrapped her sugar cube up in a ribbon so she'd have an easier time carrying it. The fairy picked up the ribbon strands and tied them to her waist before flying back out the window.

Petra tsked. "You'll never get rid of her now. She'll expect sugar every day."

Kit shrugged. "Then I'll give her sugar every day."

Petra kissed his cheek. "You're a good one, Kit. I'll leave you to your plans for the night. Pearl is staying the night with Beth, but Carina and I will both check in on her. I know you worry."

Kit wrinkled his nose. "I really do trust Ana." He

would feel better about Petra checking in on them, though.

Carina gave him an exasperated look. "You're allowed to worry about your daughter's first sleep-over. By the way, Finch sent more romances for you too. I think these are Portuguese ménages."

Kit grinned. "I knew I liked him. I'm filling my bookshelf."

Carina chuckled. "I love that they're right there next to King Nerio's books about diplomacy and historical treatises."

Petra snorted and pulled Carina with her as she left the room. "Don't let Nerio fool you. I caught him reading one of Kit's books yesterday. I've never seen that man blush so hard. It was glorious."

Kit pulled the books out of the bottom of the box and set them on the dresser. He'd enjoy looking through them later. Now, he had a romantic night to plan.

TACK LEFT HIS DAD'S OFFICE AND TOOK A MINUTE TO curse at the plant standing against the wall in the hallway. All of their scouts couldn't find a trace of Ailig and his pirates. King Ren was, understandably, upset. He was demanding answers that Nerio and Tack couldn't give him.

The man had tried to kill Kit. Of all the trouble he had caused, that was something Tack couldn't overlook.

He shook himself and started toward his rooms. It was almost dinner time, and he had a great need to see his mate.

Tack nodded to the two guards stationed at their door, then went inside. The sight of Kit in the kitchen wasn't that unusual, but Pearl and Chichi hadn't met him at the door.

"Is Pearl napping?" he asked quietly, looking toward his room.

"Nope. Her and Chichi are staying the night with Jamie and Beth at Ana's house."

Tack didn't know how he felt about that. On the one hand, he trusted Anabelle completely, but on the other hand, Pearl was his baby girl. He wanted her right beside him all the time.

Kit gave him a sympathetic look. "I know how you feel. I'm happy she has friends now, but this is hard."

Tack sat on a stool at the bar and propped his arms in front of him. "What are you doing?"

Kit grinned and swayed to the music playing from the wireless speaker hanging in the corner of the room. "I'm making dinner – lobster tail with garlic butter, broccoli, and roasted green beans. Esme made us cranachan for dessert."

Tack smiled wide. "You're still enjoying your cooking lessons?"

"Yes." Kit pumped an arm in the air and shook his butt, looking remarkably like Pearl.

Tack had noticed the longer Kit stayed with them, the more carefree he acted. He liked dancing around the room and teased everyone, regardless of class or species. Tack had even caught Kit and Leona pranking Laird Sutton the previous week.

The normally dour and uptight laird had laughed hard at the sight of the gummy worm curled up on his morning apple. The man had told Kit and Leona that they clearly needed lessons on pranking, and the three had promptly started plotting something.

"How did the meeting with Nerio go?" Kit asked as he pulled something from the oven.

Tack winced. "Not good. We still haven't found Ailig and the pirates."

"Kai said Father is getting impatient." Kit lit the candle in the middle of the table in the breakfast nook.

Tack looked around the room and noticed candles and flowers everywhere. *Odd.*

"Kai and Talia have a plan, but they won't tell me what it is." Kit dished up their plates and set them on the table. "I'd be angrier, but they aren't telling Father either. Did you get the picture Eloise sent us all?"

Eloise and Nami's daughter, Jade, had been born a few weeks ago, and Eloise had been sending pictures to everyone every five minutes.

"How did she even get my number?" Tack scowled. "She asked me if my merform has two penises and I explained they're called claspers, not penises. That was obviously a mistake because now she won't leave me alone. She keeps asking if I have two penises in my human form. Apparently, Kai stopped answering her questions about shark tailed merfolk, so she seems to think she can ask me. Why me? There's plenty of shark tailed mers in Latch Bay."

Kit snickered. "She has no boundaries. Did you see the baby?"

Tack couldn't stop his smile. "She's a cutie. Let's hope she takes after Nami. Eloise also sent me a picture of Nami and Dover riding around Latch Bay on a vespa and motorcycle."

"That's Velma and Cherry."

"They named their vehicles?" Tack shook his head.

Kit laughed again and sipped his juice. Tack's eyes roamed over the emerald green kimono and matching sarong Kit wore. He had even left off his lobster shoes for the first time since Finch had given them to him. The Napoleonic-era necklace Tack had given him encircled Kit's neck, and gold and green beads were woven through his shoulder-length red hair.

"Kit?" Tack looked down at his normal black armor. "Am I underdressed for dinner?"

Kit's cheeks flushed pink. "Sit down. We need to talk."

The blood drained from Tack's face as he fell into his seat. "What's wrong? Are you not happy?"

Kit reached out and took his gloved hand. "Nothing's wrong, Tack. I've never been happier in my life. I love my family, but it was hard living in Latch Bay. Mother was always pushing me to be different and to lose weight. Kai and Dover were wonderful, but I always felt like I was holding them back from something. Talia has always been concerned with protecting us, not really getting to know us. The others weren't horrible, well except for Lorelei, but they were never my friends."

Tack's eyes narrowed. He *really* didn't like Queen Kelby and most of Kit's siblings.

Kit's smile sent heat straight to Tack's dick. "Here, though, everything is different. I wear what I want and eat what I want. No one judges me or mocks me. I have friends, Tack." He laughed, and his bright green eyes danced with joy. "I've always kind of had Carina, but now, I really do have her. She's my friend, not my servant. I have Aber, Ana, Leona, Finch, Grace, Sutton, and so many more."

Tack breathed a little easier. "I want you to be happy."

"I know, tesoro mio, and I am." Kit watched him for a few moments, eyes soft with some emotion Tack couldn't recognize. "I have you too. You're my best friend, Tack, and my husband. I trust you to put Pearl and me first and that's not something I can reasonably say about anyone else. I know this marriage wasn't a love match or a true mating, but I can't imagine anyone I would rather be married to."

Tack pushed away the part of himself that wanted to scream in pain. He wanted Kit's love, not his friendship. *I'll take what I can get.* He reminded himself of the sight of Victoria lying dead on the rocks of Crossdows Cove.

Kit swallowed hard and his cheeks tinted pink again. "With all that said, there is something else I would like."

"Anything," Tack said, voice hoarse.

Kit snorted and sat back in his seat. "You might

want to hear me out before you agree. I want to have sex with you."

Tack's mouth opened and closed as he tried to process Kit's words. "Sex with me? The curse makes –"

"Your skin painful to touch. I know." Kit looked down at his plate. "There are other things we can do." He looked up quickly. "But only if you want to. I enjoy our time together Tack and that's enough for me. I just thought that maybe... What are you doing?"

Tack was already on his feet and behind Kit's chair. He pulled his mate's chair away from the table. "What kind of things are you talking about?"

Kit laughed. "Let's eat dinner first."

Tack scowled. "I need to hear about these things."

Kit's eyes danced, and he pointed to Tack's chair. "Sit down, tesoro mio."

Tack groaned but did as he was told. He let Kit start on his dinner and made an effort to enjoy the food his mate had cooked. It was delicious, but he suspected whatever Kit was planning for later would be better.

"We can't touch each other's skin, but there are still things we can." Kit sipped his tea. "I just want you to know that if you feel uncomfortable about anything, let me know. It's no fun if we're both not enjoying it, right?"

Tack nodded and studied Kit's lips. "I understand."

Kit smiled. "You stopped eating."

Tack took a big bite of broccoli. "So good."

Laughter filled the room and warmed something inside him. Kit shook his head. "Let's put this up to eat later. I think we both would rather be doing something else."

Tack jumped up and grabbed their plates. He set them into the refrigerator, then turned around and picked Kit up from his chair.

Kit laughed as he carried him to the bedroom. "You're ridiculous."

Tack paused and looked around the room. Kit had lit more candles and lowered the lights. Vases filled with fragrant blooms sat on every available surface. "I've never been seduced before."

Kit made a face. "I've never tried to seduce someone before. Apparently, good food, candles, and flowers aren't really needed."

Tack grinned and set Kit on his feet. "Nope. Just say the word and I'm seduced."

Kit gave him a shy look and picked up a pair of green velvet opera gloves. He pulled them on slowly. "I never thought gloves were sexy before, but every time you touch me, I swear I feel you through your gloves."

Tack's eyes followed the glide of velvet along Kit's bare skin. He had never thought gloves could be sexy either, but fuck if he couldn't wait to feel Kit's hands on him.

Kit stepped closer and cupped Tack's face in his hands. "I wish I could kiss you. Maybe if I could taste your lips one time, I wouldn't crave it so much."

He pulled the thin, silky sleeve of his kimono up and pressed it to Tack's lips before leaning forward and kissing him through the cloth. Tack's eyes closed, and he focused on the damp warmth filtering through. He pulled Kit's soft body closer and ran his hands up and down Kit's back. He loved his mate's softness.

Kit pushed back from their kiss, eyes dazed. "Is it bad that I've been jealous of Pearl? She can run up and kiss anyone she wants, but I've been hesitant to use my own kissy hanky."

Tack cupped Kit's full ass and pulled their bodies flush together. "Never hesitate to kiss me. I'll enjoy each and every kiss or touch you give me."

Kit wiggled against him, stomach pressing against Tack's hard dick. "I don't know if you understand what you're agreeing to, but I'll take it."

Tack walked them to his bed and pulled Kit onto his lap. "How are we going to do this?"

Kit moved to straddle him, his sarong parting to reveal a bare, plump thigh. "Just follow my lead, tesoro mio."

He pushed Tack back until he laid flat on the bed, then smoothed his hands down Tack's chest. "Okay, uh, I need you out of this armor. I was going to undress you all sexy-like, but does this thing even zip?"

Tack grinned and sat back up, tugging at the pieces of his armored clothing and tossing them over the side of the bed. He made sure to keep his own gloves on. He didn't want to reach for Kit in the heat of the moment and hurt him.

Kit patted his plain t-shirt. "I can handle this." He pulled it up and over Tack's head, then smoothed his gloved hands over Tack's chest.

Tack closed his eyes, feeling the prick of tears. He didn't know how to describe the sensation of Kit's touches. The velvet was warm and soft, but knowing Kit was just beneath the material, that he was the one directing the touches, was something else entirely.

Kit pushed him back again and he lay down, giving himself over to Kit's touches. His mate started at his face. He traced Tack's cheekbones and his chin. He pulled his kimono sleeve up again and gently kissed each of Tack's closed eyes.

When Kit pressed a gloved finger over Tack's lips, he couldn't resist nipping at his mate's finger. He drew it into his mouth and circled it with his tongue. The velvet didn't exactly taste pleasant, but the heat in Kit's eyes made it worth it.

Kit squeaked and pulled his finger away. He continued his exploration of Tack's skin by trailing his hands over Tack's neck, then his shoulders and arms. Kit held Tack's hands to his face and kissed the palms of his gloves before nuzzling them.

Then he moved onto Tack's chest and tweaked Tack's hardened nipples. Kit leaned down and placed his sleeve over one of Tack's nipples. He kept his eyes on Tack's face as he drew the pebbled nub into his much and sucked.

Tack moaned and his hips arched involuntarily. "Kit."

Kit gently nibbled the hard nub, then moved on to the other, taking his time to give it equal attention.

My own touch doesn't feel this good. Tack was afraid that Kit's touch was completely ruining him.

Kit freed Tack's nipples, and moved on down his stomach and hips. His fingers trailed over Tack's hard thighs, then down his legs. He nibbled on the back of Tack's knees, making him moan again.

Finally, Kit's gloved hands took hold of Tack's hard erection. One hand fondled his heavy balls while the other hand stroked him, base to tip.

Tack rested his hands on Kit's thighs and let himself soak in his mate's touch. It was almost too painful, too much pleasure. *How have I ever lived without him?*

Kit's tongue poked out of his mouth as he concentrated on making Tack come, and Tack would have laughed if he wasn't so far gone. "Kit, I'm coming."

"Good."

Tack's laugh cut off when his body bowed up and he found his release. Ropes of cum covered Kit's gloves and Tack's stomach.

Kit's heavy-lidded eyes watched him as he licked cum from his gloves. "I can taste you."

Tack groaned and rolled Kit over, laying his mate out beside him. "My turn. I want to taste you."

Kit nodded eagerly. "Yes, yes, yes."

Tack carefully removed Kit's clothes, nervous about his own bare skin being so close to Kit's. "You're so beautiful."

Kit looked down his body. "Are you drunk?"

Tack scowled. "I know what I see."

He took his time learning Kit's body. So many times he had wanted to reach out to his mate but had hesitated. *Never again.*

He used Kit's kimono to press his own kisses to Kit's face. He kissed each eyelid and plump cheek, then kissed his mate's soft, full lips.

Tack stroked a path over Kit's long neck and lightly muscled arms. He took his time with Kit's nipples, enjoying Kit's moans when he sucked and bit them.

By the time he reached Kit's soft, lightly extended stomach, Tack was hard again. He spread his hands over Kit's abdomen and used the kimono to press kisses all over the small baby bump.

As he moved down, he licked his lips. He would give anything to be able to wrap his lips around his mate's long, hard dick.

Kit wiggled in his hands and gave him a shy look. "I, um, may have used a toy today. I hoped we would get here, and now that we are, I don't know if you'd want to, um, do that with me."

Tack slowly stroked Kit's dick, loving how Kit's eyes rolled back when he did. "What toy?"

Kit panted. "I can't think when you do that."

Tack smirked and stroked him again. "I know. That's why I like doing it."

"It's in my ass," Kit said in between pants.

Tack's eyes widened and he released Kit's dick. "You have a toy inside you? Right now?"

"A butt plug." Kit bit his lip. "It feels so good."

Kit laughed as Tack flipped him over. "I have to see it."

Tack groaned at the sight of Kit's plump ass. He took his time squeezing and petting it before he parted his mate's cheeks. Sure enough, the end of an electric blue butt plug greeted him.

Tack tugged on the end of the plug and Kit

squeaked, his hands grabbing at the blankets beneath him.

"Hmm, I like this." Tack pulled the plug out, then pushed it back in. Kit arched his ass and moaned, tucking a leg beneath him.

Tack wrapped a hand around his own dick and worked it as he fucked Kit's ass with the plug. He wanted inside his mate. He wanted to feel the tight warmth of Kit's ass around him. He wanted to hold his husband in his arms and bit the back of his neck as they mated.

Kit screamed when he came and Tack splattered cum across Kit's ass.

Tack's legs shook as he waited for his breath to settle down. Kit rolled over and stared at him, eyes soft and sweet.

Tack couldn't resist swiping a drop of Kit's cum and tasting it. *Sweet and salty, just like my mate.*

"Thank you," Kit whispered, eyes sleepy. "That was even better than the heat swarm. I think it's because it was with you."

Tack bit back a moan at his words. "I've never been with anyone, Kit. I didn't even bother trying to think of ways around the curse. I would be a happy man even if I never got to come again."

Kit snorted. "Don't talk crazy. There's a whole box of dildos and vibrators in our closet. You and I both have a lot of catching up to do."

Tack sighed happily. "Perfect."

A wooden dollhouse on a table next to one of the

windows caught his eye. A fairy sat on a rocking chair on the small porch. She sipped from a tiny teacup.

"Kit, why is there a dollhouse with a fairy in it next to your napping couch?"

Kit yawned. "That's Hazelnut. She lives here now."

CHAPTER 14

*J*ack whistled as he shuffled through the pictures Hali had sent of the Día Precioso. An icy rain beat against the windows of his office, and a warm fire burned in the corner fireplace.

Pearl and Chichi played next to his desk. Well, Tack called it playing, but Chichi didn't look happy.

Pearl pulled a blue dress with white polka dots over Chichi's head and moved his legs into the holes. "Good, Chichi. You look pretty."

Tack gave the cat a sympathetic look and went back to the pictures on his tablet. The excavation was coming along nicely, and Hali was sending the first shipment of the valuables they had discovered so far.

Time to send a message to Spain. He typed out a quick e-mail to his contact in Spain and looked back over the picture of the tiny gold locket. He would need to clean it up, but he thought there was a sunbeam on the front. *It'll look good on Pearl.*

Tack and his teams only excavated shipwrecks in

international waters, and the rule of thumb was *finders keepers*. However, the treasure wasn't the only thing Tack's people found, and he preferred to give historical artifacts back to the nation they originally came from. The Día Precioso was almost intact, though without proper care, it wouldn't stay that way long.

Tack had ordered Hali to remove any treasure found, but once the excavation was complete, he would see the ship returned to Spain.

He smoothed a hand over the picture of the large hole in the hull of the ship. The evidence was pointing toward sirens. He typed out a quick message to Hali. Siren colonies sometimes kept the bones of their victims in a large, communal nest. Tack wasn't sure if there was anything left from the colony after so many years, but it couldn't hurt to check.

Tack heard a knock and looked up.

His uncle leaned against his open door. "What has you whistling?"

Tack grinned wide and shrugged. "I'm happy."

His uncle looked taken aback for a moment. "Goddess, your smiles still surprise me." His eyes softened. "Happiness looks good on you, Tack."

"Grunki Fin, look." Pearl stood up and led Chichi to Finbar. "Chichi is pretty, right?"

Chichi glared up at Finbar.

Tack's uncle hid a smile. "He's beautiful, little bit. Do you want to come visit Pappy with me? My son is suspiciously excited, so I think Tack is about to have a visitor."

She grabbed Finbar's hand and swung it. "'Kay." She waved at him. "Bye-bye, Otter Daddy."

"Have fun, little bit." Tack watched them go and waited for his *visitor*.

Seamus shuffled in, smiling wide. His cousin practically bounced in excitement. "You'll never believe what Jamalla found on the east coast."

Tack leaned forward. "The east coast? I thought we searched our coasts well already. What could be there for her to find?"

"What was the northern king doing in the twelfth century?" Seamus asked, sitting in one of the seats in front of him.

"Cleaning off the Northern Silver Isles and defending the southern border from the tentacle tailed." Tack frowned. That particular king was the one that brought the Sea Witch's curse down on the Muir family.

Seamus shook his head. "What else?"

"Getting cursed?"

Seamus rolled his eyes. "Before *that* king."

Tack thought for a moment. "King Eric spent most of his reign trying to make an alliance with the merfolk in the Mediterranean." For some reason, they hadn't been impressed with his cruelty and blatant thievery.

"Yes, that one." Seamus clapped his hands. "Remember when he sent a ship full of gold to one of the old Mediterranean families, but it disappeared?"

Tack searched on his tablet for a minute. "The ship was The Red Glory. The escort was never heard from again."

"Until now." Seamus bounced in his seat. "Jamalla found pieces of it in an underwater cave that appears to be a hydra nest."

Tack sat up straight. "A hydra? Did she go in?"

Seamus nodded. "She got some readings around the entrance and found part of the figurehead."

"Why did she do that? Hydras are at the top of the food chain." The creatures lived for centuries, and were almost indestructible.

"I told her that." Seamus chewed on his lip. "When she went in, she found the rest of the figurehead and some of the hull. She thinks there is more there."

"Any signs of the hydra being active?"

Seamus winced. "Yes, and make that *hydras*, as in more than one. She says she thought she saw signs of four or five active hydras, but she didn't want to go in further. Luckily they weren't in the cave at the moment."

"Goddess, this is bad." Tack sat back in his chair. He had never heard of more than one sharing a nest, but maybe one of the creatures had babies. "We need to take care of the nest. Where along the coast is it?"

"Close to the Deep. It's almost at our border with them."

Tack shook his head. "We don't have any towns along that part of the coast, but Laird Della often sends her fishing boats there." Merfolk had a very efficient method of fishing using spotters in the water and reelers on the boats. He would hate to see one of them attract the hydras.

"What should we do?" Seamus asked. He looked both parts worried and excited.

"Finch and I will go scout it out. That should give me an idea of how we need to deal with the nest. I don't think we have the firepower to kill even one hydra, but we might be able to entice them to relocate. At the very least, we can restrict travel to the area."

Seamus got a stubborn look on his face. "I'm coming too."

"Seamus –"

"I want to help. Someone could get hurt, and I'm trained in first aid."

Tack scowled. "Damn it. You get to be the one to tell Uncle Fin you're about to scout out a hydra nest."

Seamus gave him a smug look. "I'll tell him whatever you tell Kit."

Tack breathed out, shoulders slumping. "Damn it."

TACK STOOPED SO KIT COULD GIVE HIM A KISS THROUGH the thin handkerchief. "Thank you for lending us your boat."

Finch choked on a laugh. "Yes, Kit. Thank you so much for lending us the *TacKit*. We'll be the envy of the ocean."

Kit smiled happily. "It's a good boat and it's too cold for you all to be swimming so far. Seamus and I packed plenty of snacks and drinks, but are you sure you need to go fishing right now?"

Tack pulled Kit's coat tighter around his large baby

bump. He was six months along now, and Tack thought he was the most beautiful creature in the world. "Thank you for the snacks, sweetling. If you made them, I know they'll be delicious."

"What about the weather?" Kit looked up at the grey sky.

"A little icy rain won't hurt us," Seamus added, laughing nervously. His eyes darted around for Finbar. "We'll be back before you know it."

"You needs to take Chichi?" Pearl asked and pointed to her pet. Luca currently carried the massive cat since Pearl didn't wanted Chichi's paws to get cold. Tack thought Chichi and Luca looked remarkably alike with their disgusted expressions. *At least Luca isn't wearing a plaid onesie like the cat.*

"I think Chichi needs to stay with you, little bit." Tack knelt down and hugged her. Pearl squeezed him tight and gave him a kiss with her hanky.

Kit nibbled on his lip. "Pearl and I will be here when you get back. I'll cook up whatever you catch."

"Thanks, Kit." Finch bowed low. "You're my favorite royal, you know."

Tack grabbed Finch by the back of the neck and pulled him toward the boat. "We'll be back in about a week."

A few minutes later, he watched Kit and Pearl wave at them from the docks. Guards surrounded his family, but Tack hated leaving them behind.

Finch patted his shoulder. "They'll be alright. I told my lieutenant that you'd feed him to Lola if anything happened to them."

Lola chose that moment to swim by the boat. Betty and Veronica swam on either side of her. Sometimes Tack thought they liked to taunt the great white shark.

Eat seals? Lola sent an image of herself munching on Seamus's seals.

You know the answer to that.

Hungry.

You can hunt at the feeding reefs.

Tack could almost feel the shark's sigh when Veronica bumped Lola's tail with her nose.

THEY WERE ONLY A DAY INTO THEIR TRIP WHEN SEAMUS'S seals barked nervously from where they sat on the swimming platform of the boat. Tack focused on Lola, and his companion sent him back an image of several tentacle tailed merfolk heading their way.

"We have company coming." Tack checked his weapons and sent a quick text to the castle with their coordinates.

Seamus took the helm, and Finch joined him, face cold and fingers tapping the gun holstered to his chest. "Who is it?"

"The tentacle tailed."

A few moments later, a familiar face poked above the water. Sea Witch Johanna's eyes were hard, all traces of friendliness and laughter gone. Her long white hair hung in braids and she wore a winged helmet of gold instead of her crown.

Over fifty tentacle tailed merfolk surfaced behind

her, faces equally grim. Her apprentice, Marlowe, swam at her side, face emotionless.

More from the deep. Lola sent him an image of hundreds of more tentacle tailed merfolk waiting below.

"What's wrong?" Tack asked, getting straight to the point. He truly didn't think she would attack for no reason.

She raised an arm above water and held up a severed head. "Do you recognize this merman?"

"Fuck." Finch startled, then steadied, reaching for his gun.

Tack grabbed his arm, stilling him. "Finch, that man looks familiar. Do you recognize him?"

Finch made a face but leaned closer, eyes narrowed. "He does look familiar."

"That was one of Ailig's men," Seamus said from the helm. His cousin looked pale and his eyes were glued to the head. "I remember him because he almost got on the boat. Finch knocked him in the head and he fell back into the water. I haven't seen him since."

Johanna tossed the head onto their boat, and Betty and Veronica galumphed across the deck to hide behind Seamus. "He wore a Coalswell guard uniform and led over a hundred merfolk into *my* waters. They attacked a hippocampi herd."

"How many did they kill?" Tack asked, voice grim.

"None." She raised her arms and the water surrounding her formed six tentacles. They wrapped around the boat and lifted it from the water. "I guard the Deep well."

Finch cursed and drew his gun, aiming it at Johanna, and the tentacle tailed soldiers drew their weapons as well.

Marlowe just looked bored.

Tack held out his hands. "It wasn't us. We've had problems with a pirate named Ailig. He ambushes our merchant ships and excavation teams. He even attacked Kit when he was on the way to Coalswell Tides."

Johanna gave him a hard look, but her water tentacles settled the boat back into the water. "Take a swim with me. We'll talk."

Finch snorted. "Not likely, Sea Witch."

Tack pulled his boots and pants off and vaulted into the water, summoning his tail. He saw the tentacle tailed army below. Underwater they were even more intimidating.

CHAPTER 15

S ea Witch Johanna's long black tentacles moved her gracefully through the water at a speed Tack hadn't expected. She was suddenly right beside him, expression grim. Two black eels twisted around her and glared at him.

He watched them thoughtfully. *We aren't the only ones with companions.*

"Damn it, Tack." Finch jumped in behind him and shifted into his Kelpie form.

Seamus gave the tentacle tailed army a considering look from the boat. "Betty, Veronica, and I will stay here and guard the snacks."

Marlowe looked interested. "What kind of snacks?"

Tack heard Seamus speaking with Marlowe, but didn't pay attention. He shoved Finch toward the boat. "Guard Seamus."

Finch snorted and headbutted his shoulder and refused to go.

"Your cousin will be safe. Follow me." Johanna

swam under their boat and headed toward the rocky cliffs of the eastern coast of the kingdom.

A large, dark-skinned tentacle tailed soldier followed them, and Finch fell back to swim behind the merman, eying him suspiciously. Tack let some of his tension drain. The soldier was well-armed and looked battle tested, but Tack had every faith in Finch's skills.

"That's Kristoff." Johanna waved to the soldier. "My general."

He pointed at Finch. "That's Finch, my personal assistant."

Finch snorted and glared at him.

Johanna gave Tack a small smile. "Why are you so far from Coalswell Tides? I didn't expect to meet you here."

"There's a hydra nest near our border. We need to scout it out and figure a way to get rid of it."

"It's been there for as long as I can remember. A few hundred years ago, the hydra that made the nest laid four eggs. She left after they were born to make a new nest, and the four hatchlings have lived there ever since." She frowned. "The hippocampi know to avoid them, so the four feed on sharks, squids, and the occasional whale. They tend to keep away from merfolk and ships."

"How do you know that?" he asked, watching her closely. He didn't like that she knew more about the seas in his kingdom than he did.

Water swirled behind them and carried the group quickly to where Lola swam closer to shore. "As the Sea Witch, I know all that lies in the sea."

"Hydras are solitary creatures. Why are they staying together?" Tack asked.

Johanna shrugged. "I'm not about to go ask them. If anything in the sea can kill the Sea Witch, it's a hydra." She gave him an expectant look. "Now, the hydras will wait. Tell me about these pirates."

"Ailig used to be a laird." Tack stroked a hand down Lola's back when she swam close beside him. "He hates the royal family, so he left. About three years ago, he returned with a large number of pirates. They began attacking our ships and excavation teams but were easy enough to beat back. The last year has been different. They've attacked a couple of our coastal towns, and their numbers seem to be increasing every time we fight with them. We suspect they're working with someone with money or connections."

"Where are they?" Johanna asked and let one of her eels wrap itself around her arm. "I'll take care of them now that they've attacked the Deep."

Dad would just love that, Tack thought. Nerio wanted no help from either Ren or Johanna. "We don't know. We've searched everywhere but can't find them."

"Their base can't be in the seas or I would sense them." She frowned in concentration, eyes distant.

The crash of waves against the cliffs soothed Tack, and he took a moment to look around. Much of the east coast was wild seas and sheer cliffs. Underwater, the currents were strong, and the water ebbed and flowed. He let his body drift with the water.

"Nothing." Johanna scowled. "I truly can't sense them."

"Did you sense the attack on my husband?" Tack asked, curious.

"Yes." She swam down toward the bottom of the cliff.

Tack growled and followed her. "Why didn't you use your magic to stop it? Merfolk died during the attack."

Johanna gave him a sad look, then turned to Kristoff. "Stay here with the Kelpie. I have something I need to show Prince Tack."

Kristoff nodded, but Finch snorted and shook his head.

"Finch, please stay." Tack gave him a look. "Keep an eye on the general. We don't know him."

Kristoff raised a brow. Tack suspected he knew he was being used to make Finch listen.

Johanna linked her arm with his, surprising him. Few besides those closest to Tack chanced getting close to him. "Come along."

They swam a short distance through the kelp growing along the sandy bottom of the ocean.

Johanna's lips were a thin line in her pale face. She rolled the long strand of black pearls she wore around her neck. "Millenia before Sea Witch Adriane cursed your family, a great evil walked the land. This evil being created four powerful monsters to do its bidding."

Tack gave her a puzzled look. "An evil being? Seriously? What was its bidding?"

"The destruction of the world." Johanna gave him a hard look. "This is important, so listen. One of the creatures was charged with destroying the seas and all those that lived within it, so the Goddess entrusted her most powerful water witch with the power of the seas. That witch became the first Sea Witch."

"Okay?" Tack could tell that Johanna believed every word she spoke, so he tried to hold back his sarcasm.

"The Sea Witch fought the water creature, but could not kill it. Instead, with the Goddess's help, he imprisoned it within the Deep. When his apprentice was born, he transferred some of his power to her and trained her to wield both water magic and the power of the seas. Together, they guarded the creature and did their best to protect the world. That has been the duty bestowed to every Sea Witch since the first."

Tack licked his lips. "Your apprentice is Sea Witch Marlowe."

"Yes." Johanna nodded. "The power of the seas *should* be split evenly between Marlowe and myself."

"Should?"

"When Sea Witch Adriane cursed your two families, the anger and hatred she sent displeased the Goddess and the sea. While she was justified in her vengeance, she did more than harm the two men that betrayed her."

"She's harmed hundreds now."

"More than that." Johanna pulled him further along the shore. "Our beautiful city sank to the bottom of the ocean as all her power was thrust onto her poor apprentice as she died. When Adriane cursed the Muir and Rees families, she lost the Goddess's trust and we were cursed as well."

Tack's eyes widened. "Your people are cursed? What's the curse?"

Johanna looked away for a moment. "It's nothing for you to worry about. The true problem is that within the past fifty years or so, something has been siphoning the Sea Witches' magic. There are only ever two Sea Witches. When Marlowe's apprentice is born, I'll transfer all my power to Marlowe, and he will give portions of it to his apprentice as he trains the child. That is our cycle, but something is interfering with it. My own master noticed the change, but we've never been able to find the source. I suspect it's related to the curse, but I don't know."

"So you and Marlowe are weaker than you should be." Tack pressed his lips into a hard line. Johanna's demonstration of power earlier had been impressive, and that was her when she was weakened.

"Yes." Johanna sighed. "Our priority is to guard the creature's prison. While I have more than enough power to protect the Deep, I cannot extend myself often."

"Are you saying that was why you couldn't help during the attack on Kit?" Tack shook his head angrily. "I don't believe there's some ancient monster in the Deep. I think you created a convoluted story to avoid admitting you don't care enough about the other kingdoms to help fight an enemy that's not your own. There's no reason to lie. It's not as if King Ren or my dad would offer you aid either."

Johanna thumped his arm. "I *do* care, you dolt. I actually like you and the others. Marlowe and I truly don't hold as much power as we should. As for the creature, I'd just as soon you never had to worry about believing it's there."

Tack narrowed his eyes. "Let's say you're telling the truth. Why would you tell me your weakness?"

She watched him for a moment, then pulled him to the cliff. "Look here."

He followed her finger and saw a tiny creature clinging to the rock. Its small body was pushed back and forth with the current.

"Is that a… No." Tack shook his head. "It can't be."

"It's a water dragonling." Johanna gave him a sad look. "Dragonlings are so rare. This one was abandoned by his mother when he didn't take to flying as quickly as her other hatchlings."

"Damn it, he looks weak." Tack swam forward and gently pried the little dragonling's claws from the rock. The creature was about the size of one of Pearl's dolls. Its scales varied from dark blue to white, and the poor creature's deep blue eyes were full of fear and exhaustion.

"The weak do not survive in the sea," Johanna said. "It would make a snack for your shark."

Snack? Lola swam to them.

"No, Lola." Tack glared at Johanna and pulled up some kelp to wrap the dragonling in. "I'll take him back to Kit. He'll raise him up like the damn mother should have. You don't sacrifice your weak because they're inconvenient."

Johanna smiled wide, eyes glittering in the light of the filtered sun. "That's why I'm telling you about my weakness. Through the sea, I've watched you and your cousins for a long time, Tack. I was with you when you bonded with Lola. Your father and uncle were petrified when you didn't try for one of the younger sharks. You saw Lola and knew she was meant to be your companion. Your grandfather held them back, and we all watched as you bonded her. I see Hali now, working so hard to make you and Finbar proud. When you gave her the responsibility of that excavation, you gave her the chance she needed to prove her worth to the Muir family. I watch my darling Seamus often as he swims about searching for his place in this world. He has a beautiful heart, Tack. Each of you do."

Tack floated listlessly, shocked at her words. "You watch us? That's kind of creepy."

She snickered. "Being creepy is part of the Sea Witch job description."

Tack shook his head. "Okay. I understand why you couldn't help then. Honestly, Dad and King Ren both would have been upset if you had."

She rolled her eyes. "They're just as stubborn as you are."

Tack frowned and cradled the dragonling. "I'm not stubborn. I'm here speaking with you instead of starting a war because you brought an army into our kingdom."

Johanna took his arm, and they started back toward where Finch and Kristoff waited. "If you aren't stubborn, then why haven't you told Kit that he's your mate?"

Tack pulled her to a stop. "How do you know that?"

She gave him a disbelieving look. "I just told you I watch you often. I'd have to be an idiot not to see it."

Panic filled him, and Tack's tail thrashed back and forth. "He can't know. I don't want him to die like Victoria."

"Tack, your situation is entirely different than your uncle's."

"No." Tack glared at her. "This is my decision, not yours, and I won't risk it. I'll spend my life making Kit happy and the curse can just fuck off."

Johanna groaned. "Men are so stupid."

Tack pulled her along with him as he swam. "You know, Kit mentioned he thought you said there were three curses. The Rees family, the Muir family, and the Sea Witch."

She tilted her chin up and narrowed her eyes on him. "That is none of your concern. Curses can just *fuck off*, right?"

"Sea Witch –"

She patted his arm. "Take your dragonling back to your mate. Marlowe and I need to get back to the Deep before the damn Leviathan escapes and destroys the world."

Tack blinked and stopped swimming again. "Leviathan?"

CHAPTER 16

"*A*re you sure she said *Leviathan*?" Seamus asked. He sat on the swimming platform with Betty and Veronica.

"I swear that's what she said." Tack fed the dragonling another bit of the smoked salmon Kit had packed for them. The little guy gulped it down, then watched him with wide eyes before opening his mouth again. Tack gave him another bite.

"Son of a bitch," Finch yelled from the front of the boat. He was at the helm, steering them back to Coalswell Tides. "Tack, I just got a call from Petra. She said King Ren and his mates arrived at the castle in a helicopter. They brought a shit ton of Latch Bay guards. They're demanding King Nerio hand Kit and Pearl over to them. Petra said they claim we attacked one of their pearl farms."

"Fucking Ailig." Tack handed the dragonling to Seamus and hurried to grab the microphone for the boat's radio. His hands shook as he put it to his mouth. "Petra?"

"Prince Tack, there's a mess brewing." He didn't like that she sounded so shaken. "King Ren has a video of our people attacking one of the pearl farms. Twenty-six guppy-tails were murdered before the attackers were taken out."

"It's Ailig. Tell Dad to read the damn report I sent him. They're disguising themselves as us and attacking our allies. The Sea Witch killed a group of them in the Deep."

"Nerio read the report, Tack. King Ren doesn't believe him."

"We're an hour away." Tack took a deep breath, trying to ignore the ball of ice building in his chest. "Please don't let them take my sweetling and our daughter, Petra."

She gasped. "Oh, Tack. It's like that, is it?"

Finch watched him carefully.

Tack looked away. "Yes. I love him."

Petra growled. "I'll protect Kit. They'll only take him over my dead body. Get home fast and let's figure this shit out."

"Yes, ma'am." He set the microphone back in place. "How fast can this boat go?"

Finch grinned wickedly. "Let's find out."

They arrived in Latch Bay in forty minutes. Seamus took over the helm and Finch and Tack jumped into the water, shifting forms to swim through the lower castle so they could reach Kit faster.

The dragonling was a warm weight in the sarong

tied across his chest. His head poked out and he studied everything they passed. The reefs were oddly quiet. The waters were cold, but that never kept the Nereids or northern merfolk from their swims.

Guards surrounded the castle, their grim faces telling Tack all he needed to know. *We're about to go to war.*

They quickly made their way through the lower castle and up the staircase. Tack didn't bother to find dry clothing and Finch tugged clothes on as they ran down the hallway. The dragonling chirped, then ducked its head back into its makeshift sling.

There were no servants in the hallways and the guards all nodded toward the throne room. Tack skidded into the room and came to a halt.

King Ren and King Fergus were as close to Nerio as the guards would let them. Both men looked furious. Nerio and Finbar looked equally angry and each man yelled loudly, their actual words drowned out by the others' voices.

Queen Kelby had her arm wrapped around Kit and was clearly trying to tug him toward the large group of Latch Bay guards. "Come along, Kit. This place isn't safe for you. Goddess, what are you even wearing? You're a prince, darling and you need to at least try to look like one."

"He looks just fine, you vile woman." Petra tugged on Kit's other arm, trying to pull him to the safety of the Coalswell guards. "He belongs here."

Laird Sutton and Leona glared at Kelby and looked

ready to attack the queen, while Carina stood with Grace who and held Pearl in her arms.

Weapons weren't drawn yet, but Tack could tell it would be a matter of minutes before chaos descended.

"Enough," Tack yelled and the room grew silent. "This mess is exactly what Ailig wants. Let's sit down and discuss this like the adults we are."

"Otter Daddy." Pearl scrambled out of Carina's arms. She ran to him and he bent, picking her up and putting her on his hip.

Her lip trembled, but she pulled her hanky out and kissed his cheek. "Granddaddy, Grandpop, and Grandma are being mean. They say we have to go with them. I don't want to leave."

"Don't worry, little bit." Tack stroked her cheek. "We'll figure everything out. Why don't you, Grace, and Carina go swim in the garden?"

"'Kay." She held her arms out to Carina. "Come on. Let's swim."

Carina chuckled. "Yes, ma'am."

Kelby glared at him as they left. "Pearl's coming home. You Coalswells are traitorous bastards and my son and granddaughter won't be left in your care."

Tack narrowed his eyes. "Watch your damn –"

"No." Kit wrenched his arm from Kelby's grasp and patted Petra's hand until she let him go. He ran to Tack's side and tucked himself under Tack's arm. "Tesoro mio, what's strapped to your chest? Did you catch a fish? Do northerners carry them that way?"

"Uh, not exactly."

The dragonling poked its head out and Kit gasped,

eyes lighting up. "Is that a water dragonling? Aren't they close to extinction? I've never seen one before."

"His mother abandoned him. I knew you would want to take care of him," Tack said gruffly, flushing as everyone stared at them.

Kit squealed and danced in place. "Yes, of course I do."

"Kit, calm yourself," Kelby said, looking horrified. "Princes don't squeal."

Tack growled, ready to feed the woman to Lola.

Petra cut him off when she shoved Kelby. "He's our prince and he can fucking squeal if he wants to."

"How dare you?" Kelby snarled. "I'll have your head for touching me."

"Mother, stop." Kit gave her a hard look. "This isn't your kingdom. You're a guest in Petra's castle. You all are, yet you've been nothing but disrespectful. Now, sit the fuck down and we'll talk about this."

Tack's attention caught on Ren's face. The king watched Kit, pride filling his eyes.

Fergus rushed over to Kelby, grabbing her hand. "Kit, I'm sure your mother didn't mean to upset you."

Kit narrowed his eyes. "Do I need to repeat myself?"

Kelby looked shocked. "Kit."

"Mother, I love you, but I'm done with this conversation." Kit stroked the dragonling's head. "I have more important things to do today than listen to you all yell at one another. I haven't seen Tack in almost two days and it's been horrible without him."

Tack stroked his cheek. "I missed you too, sweetling."

Abernathy and Earl came into the room. "Hey, what's with all the yelling? Does someone need a drink?"

"They could *all* use a drink, Aber." Kit pointed toward the door. "Everyone move your asses to Nerio's study."

Nerio chuckled. "You've been hanging around Petra too long."

Kit blew Nerio a kiss. "She said I'm her second in command now."

"Damn right, you are, sweetheart." Petra patted Kit's cheek.

Ren shook his head in wonder but stayed quiet.

A few moments later, Finch watched over the guards outside Nerio's study while the royal families and Petra filed inside.

Tack helped Kit unwrap the dragonling while everyone found a seat. The little creature hopped straight to Kit and climbed to his shoulder. He curled against Kit's neck and closed his eyes.

"I can't believe his mother abandoned him," Kit whispered. "My mother is a pain in the ass, but at least I know she *does* love me."

"I heard that," Kelby said dryly, arms crossed.

"Good," Nerio bit out.

Tack took a deep breath. "Alright, we need to figure out what the hell is going on before war erupts and Ailig and whoever the hell he's allying himself with takes over."

"That's their goal, isn't it?" Ren pulled at the collar

of his coat. All of the Latch Bay mers looked uncomfortable in the warmer clothing they wore.

"You believe him?" Kelby glared at her husband.

Kit sat down in the window seat, moving aside one of his romances, and grabbed one of his favorite blankets. Petra tended to keep them all over the castle in case Kit got cold. "Mother, the Coalswells aren't capable of the level of betrayal that you're accusing them of. They're good and honest people. Nerio is a wonderful king who takes care of his people. Fin makes sure the economy stays stable and flush. Aber is too busy making his whisky to try to stir up a war between us, and then there's my Tack. He's sweet and kind. He would never attack my family, and the Southern Silver Isles is my family."

Tack gave Kit a flat look. "Sweet and kind?"

Kit grinned. "Just accept it and move on, tesoro mio."

Ren nodded, face solemn. "I've heard so much about Prince Tack's sweet and kind nature."

Nerio sighed dramatically. "I worry it will affect his reign when I retire. He'll just try to hug all our enemies and give away all the kingdom's money."

Fergus's snicker cut off when Kelby glared at him. "So, moving on. How do we know for sure those weren't your people?"

Silence filled the room. Tack truly couldn't think of a way to make them believe him. He could have Johanna talk to them, but they didn't trust her either.

Abernathy stood and grabbed classes from the bar

against the far wall. "Let's have a glass and think on it, huh?"

Fergus looked hopeful. "Do you have any Abernathy Original?"

"Sure do, kiddo." Abernathy poured drinks and passed glasses around. "So, how do we do this? You don't trust us, and we don't like you."

Seamus slipped into the room and held an icebox up. "So, I have that head the Sea Witch gave us. Do you all need it?"

"You have a head in there?" Kelby pressed her hand to her heart.

"Really, son, did you need to bring that in here?" Petra asked, wincing.

Seamus shrugged. "She tossed it at us, so I thought it might be important. Tack just wanted to give it to Lola."

Finbar rubbed his forehead. "Put it in the corner, son."

"Damn, you'd think no one here has ever seen a severed head." Seamus set it down, then sat on Kit's other side.

Ren winced. "Alright. Let's assume that we can trust you Coalswells. If you're right, this Ailig and his allies want us to fight. Are they truly after our thrones?"

Tack linked his fingers with Kit's. "Right now, we are both powerful and stable kingdoms. War between us would be rough. Our resources would quickly diminish and we'd lose a lot of people. It's not too much of a stretch to think Ailig would take advantage of that to try and overthrow Dad. I don't know what he wants from the Southern Silver Isles."

"Have Kai and Talia made any progress in their plan?" Kit asked.

"What plan?" Nerio asked.

Ren gave them all a sour look. "My daughter and son have some convoluted plan to figure out where the pirate base is. They refuse to tell me what it is. I don't remember being so difficult when I was their age."

Nerio grunted. "I can empathize. My brilliant son decided to go scout out a hydra nest without telling anyone."

"He did what?" Kit's head whipped to the side and his eyes narrowed. "You weren't going on a fishing trip?"

Tack sunk in the window seat. "I didn't want you to worry, sweetling."

"Don't you *sweetling* me, Tack Muir. You're sleeping on the couch for the foreseeable future."

Finbar glared at Seamus. "What the hell were you thinking, Shay? You're a cook, not a monster hunter."

Seamus sniffed. "They would probably have needed someone to patch them up, and I can do that."

"You're not helping," Tack said dryly.

The door to Nerio's study banged open, and more of the Rees family and their friends and pets poured inside.

He scowled. *Eloise.*

Through the chaos of voices, Tack noticed Kit's brother-in-law looking around the room. Ben carried Shawn on his hip and had his chicken, Rachael, tucked under his arm. "King Nerio, I brought the piece you commissioned. It will look good on the wall behind your desk."

Nerio preened when Ren, Fergus, and Kelby all glared at him. "Thank you, Ben."

Petra frowned. "Why are you carrying a chicken?"

Fergus leaned toward her and whisper-yelled. "Humans are weird."

Tack watched Ben's dog, Otis, wander over to Abernathy. His grandfather grinned and scratched the golden doodle's ears. "Oh, you're a pretty boy. Do you want to meet Earl?"

"Dover!" Kit squealed next to Tack's ear, making him wince. The dragonling startled away and clung to Kit's shoulder.

"Look who I brought." Dover held Prue in his arms while his otter companion stretched across his shoulders.

"Tack, help me up," Kit ordered. Seamus pushed while Tack pulled until Kit was on his feet. He ran to his brother, arms outstretched.

"Kit, it's unseemly to –" Petra's glare cut Kelby off.

Eugenia wrinkled her nose. "Are you wearing lobster slippers and an orange kimono?"

"Shut your face, dillweed." Kit hugged Dover and Prue. "Look at my favorite niece."

"She's your only niece," Dover said, laughing.

"Hush, irmãozinho, and let me enjoy her." Kit kissed the top of Prue's head.

"Eloise, why didn't you bring Jade?" Kit pouted. "I haven't gotten to hold her yet."

Eloise shrugged and let out a deep breath. "You know how Nami is. She didn't want me to bring the baby to enemy territory."

"Unlike us, who take Shawn and Prue everywhere," Dover said, laughing.

"We know they're not enemies," Ben said, bouncing Shawn on his hip. He set Rachael down and the chicken started inspecting the room.

The noise level grew and Eloise sat in Kit's spot beside Tack. She patted his knee. "So, about those penises."

Tack groaned. "I swear, beaver, I'll feed you to Lola if you don't stop asking me questions about my penis."

"Oh, I see." Eloise leaned back. "Penis as in singular. Does that mean you just have one in human form? How big is it?"

Seamus chuckled. "You know my father and Uncle Nerio are also shark tailed mers, right?"

Eloise's eyes zeroed in on Finbar and she smiled wide. "This will be fun." She jumped up and went straight to Finbar.

Tack fist bumped Seamus. "I love you, Shay."

"You know I enjoy seeing my dad uncomfortable." Seamus's eyes strayed to where Kai and Talia were whispering to one another. "I could use the distraction."

Eugenia drew his attention before he could ask Seamus what he meant. She held her phone up and took a picture. "Seriously, Kit. You're even wearing a crown with that outfit. I'm sending this to Lorelei. She'll be so mad she didn't come."

Kit patted his crown. "Isn't it beautiful? Nerio picked it out of the treasury for me. He said I needed a crown as bright as I am."

Tack smiled softly. Kit's official crown was burnished gold with a variety of gems and seashells covering it. It was a clash of color and styles, but somehow, it was perfectly Kit. His mate wore it everywhere.

"Whoa, is that a water dragonling sleeping on your shoulder?" Dover gasped. "Chubber look. Isn't it cute?"

Chubber cocked his head for a moment, then jumped off Dover's shoulder and ran to Tack. The otter climbed up his leg to his lap and chirped at him angrily.

Tack gave the otter a confused look. "Should I say I'm sorry I brought the dragonling here?"

Kit snickered. "Chubber, it's just a baby."

Talia whistled to get everyone's attention. "We have something to tell you."

"Oh?" Ren crossed his arms. "Is this about the secret plan you refused to share with your sovereign ruler?"

"Yep." Kai grinned and sat next to Seamus. "We have someone on the inside of Ailig's group."

Nerio's eyes widened. "Do they know where the base is?"

"Not yet," Eugenia said, taking another picture of Kit as he cooed over Prue.

"Who is it?" Abernathy asked and fluffed Otis's ears, before going in for a thorough scratch again.

"We aren't saying." Talia gave them a stubborn look. "I won't compromise them. However, we've learned that Ailig's ally is the former lord Eades."

"What?" Ren growled. "That son of a bitch is still trying to take my throne."

Eugenia shook her head. "And you wanted me to marry his annoying son."

"We've apologized about that already, darling." Kelby sighed. "I suppose this gives credence to the Coalswells' story. This type of subterfuge is exactly something Eades would plan."

"He has no money," Fergus said thoughtfully. "How can they hire so many mercenaries to fight alongside Ailig's pirates?"

"They have the backing of one of our business competitors in the Pacific." Kai shrugged. "The Morey clan wants more control of the pearl market."

"Well then, maybe they should grow better pearls," Kelby said, standing. She paced around the room. "This is ridiculous. We have to stop them." She paused when she saw the book sitting next to the window seat. "Goddess help me, Kit. Is this one of those trashy romances I keep having to take from you? You're twenty-eight years old, darling. Read something more appropriate."

Nerio drew himself up, every inch the cold and regal king of the Northern Silver Isles. "That happens to be a very good book, Queen Kelby. I enjoyed it immensely when I read it last week."

The book fell from Kelby's hands, and she stared at Nerio in amazement. "Seriously?"

Tack picked the book up and set it back in its spot. Kit wouldn't like his precious books lying on the floor. Apparently, neither would Tack's dad.

Talia whistled again. "Back on track, folks. We're working on finding the location of Ailig and Eades' base, but it will take a little time."

"Could we maybe ask the Sea Witch to help?" Ben asked. "She can scry for a location, right?"

"Absolutely not." Ren shook his head. "We don't need to be indebted to the Deep."

"She can't find them anyway." Tack rubbed the back of his neck. "She says they must not be in the water since she can't sense them."

Nerio looked pissed. "You asked for her help?"

"No," Tack said. "She volunteered the information. Plus, like it or not, her people were attacked too. They're part of this now."

"We don't need them," Kelby said. "This is something our kingdoms can work together to figure out."

"Agreed." Nerio's smile was strained. "Petra, will you see that some rooms are readied for our guests? Since they're here already, I know Kit would enjoy a couple of days with his parents and siblings."

Ren snorted. "Smooth, Nerio. Order us to stay to appease Kit, but also tell us we'll need to get the hell out in two days."

Nerio shrugged. "Exactly."

Rachael jumped on Nerio's desk and squawked.

Nerio glared at Ben's pet. "Petra, also tell Esme not to cook the human's chicken. It might upset Kit."

CHAPTER 17

*K*it pulled Tack down the halls to their room. Now that the crisis was averted, he couldn't ignore the black edge of panic that gripped him. "A hydra nest, Tack? Those are literally the most dangerous sea creatures in the world. I haven't heard of anyone actually managing to kill one except in myths. Smart people just avoid their nests and hunting grounds."

"We were just scouting," Tack started then stopped when Kit glared at him. "I truly am sorry, sweetling. I should have just told you."

Kit stopped and turned to him, steadying the dragonling on his shoulder. "You shouldn't have tried anything so dangerous to begin with. I can't bear the thought of you being hurt. Pearl and I need you at our side, tesoro mio. I even need your damn snores to lull me to sleep. I didn't sleep at all why you were away."

He rubbed his eyes, trying not to cry. He knew he sounded like a needy, selfish brat, but he had missed

Tack so much. The dragonling chirped his ear and nuzzled against him. *My sweet little blueberry.*

Tack cupped his cheeks in his gloved hands and wiped the stray tear that fell. "I'm sorry, Kit. I really am. I didn't want you to worry, but that's no real excuse."

"It's just the damn hormones." Kit sniffled. "You know they're all over the place."

Tack's gentle smile sent a rush of heat through Kit. He had *really* missed his husband. For years Kit had gone without sex, but now that he'd felt Tack's touch, such as it was, he almost craved the man.

Tack wrapped his arms around Kit. "Let's go lock the door and snuggle with Pearl on the couch, sweetling. I missed you two, and I thought I'd lose my mind when Petra told me they were taking you two away."

"I wouldn't have left you."

"I know that now." Tack's voice grew rough. "You stood up for us and defended us against your family. You have no idea how much that means to me."

Kit pressed his face against Tack's chest. "What about my family? They're here to visit."

"They're settling in now, and we'll see them at dinner." Tack let him go, then guided him toward their door. "You look exhausted."

Kit scowled. "I've had no fucking sleep, Tack. Weren't you listening?"

"Let's fix that."

"Kit?" Fergus hurried down the hall. "I forgot to do something when we arrived."

Kit sniffled again and stroked the dragonling's head

while he waited for his omega father to catch up. "What did you forget?"

Fergus pulled him into his arms and hugged him tight.

Kit sighed and sunk into the embrace. He buried his nose against his father's neck and breathed in his familiar scent. "I missed you."

"I've missed you too, son." Fergus kissed the side of his head. "Ren and I are so proud of you for standing up for yourself. The moment Prince Tack arrived, and I saw the way you reacted, I knew we were wrong." He leaned closer, whispering. "You've found your treasure."

Kit smiled against Fergus's shoulder. "Yes, I have."

A FEW HOURS LATER, KIT STOOD AT THE FORMAL DINNER table with Esme and Seamus. All of the visitors from Latch Bay sat on one side of the table while all the Coalswells sat on the other.

"Tonight, we have baked lobster tails and honey glazed salmon for the main course." Kit bounced on the tip of his toes. "I made the salmon by myself."

Kelby gave Nerio a disdainful look. "You force my son to cook like a common servant?"

Laird Sutton growled. "King Nerio doesn't force our Kit to do anything he doesn't want to. Kit happens to love cooking and is very good at it."

Kit smiled. He really did like the grouchy laird. The man was fluent in every language Kit knew and spoke with him often. He also thought of the best pranks.

Kelby arched a brow. "Did I give you leave to address me?"

Leona tilted the pitcher of wine she carried and a few drops fell onto Kelby's lap. "Oh no, this pitcher is just so heavy."

Kelby glared at Kit's friend and dabbed at her damp dress. "Why have they not fired you."

Earl barked from his seat next to Kelby. Abernathy's companion wore the old man's crown perched on his head.

"Why must I sit next to the sea lion?" Kelby frowned at Earl. "Why is it even at the table. What kind of castle do you run, Petra?"

Petra's smile was serene as she cut into her salmon. "Oh, Earl is always welcome at our table, Queen Kelby. It's just the way things are here."

Abernathy snorted, but didn't say anything when Petra glared at him.

Fergus looked at the kids' table longingly. "Can't I go sit with Pearl and her friends?"

Ren snickered. "Sorry, but if I have to stay here, so do you."

"Those two get to sit with them." Fergus pouted and pointed at Carina and Anabelle.

The two women were laughing as they watched Beth and Pearl try to feed Shawn a tator tot through his nose. Jamie grabbed it and put it out of Shawn's reach before giving the toddler a fresh one to chew on.

"That does look like the fun table," Ren said sadly.

Kit cleared his throat. "Enjoy the meal." He hurried to his seat next to Tack. His husband's hand settled on his leg and Kit's nerves steadied.

Kai took a big bite of the salmon and groaned. "Kit, this is really good."

"You think so?" Kit looked around the table. Each of his family members had chosen the salmon. "Seamus and Esme taught me."

Kai gave Tack's cousin a half-smile. "You like to cook?"

Seamus flushed red. "Yes, I always have."

"Goddess, this *is* good." Kelby patted her mouth with her napkin. "I still say cooking isn't a good hobby to pursue, darling, but you do it very well."

Kit rolled his eyes. "Thank you, Mother."

Earl leaned over and stuck his face in Kelby's plate.

She gave Petra a flat look as the rest of the table laughed at her. "Dare I ask for another plate?"

THE NEXT MORNING, KIT LEFT PEARL TO VISIT WITH HER cousins and grandparents. He wanted some time with his brothers and sisters while they were here. Over four months had passed since he left Latch Bay, and phone calls and video chats weren't enough.

"I can't believe they built this for you," Dover said, shaking his head as they left the garden. "They even call it Kit's Garden."

Eloise wrapped an arm around Tack's shoulders and made kissy faces. "It's 'cause *TacKit* is the real deal.

C.W. GRAY

The big and brooding northern prince really is a soft, mushy romantic."

Kit had to cover his mouth to keep from laughing at Tack's expression. His husband really didn't like Eloise.

Seamus chuckled. He walked with Kai at the back of the group, so Kit barely heard him. "I think at first, Tack didn't realize his shark wouldn't eat Kit. He just wanted him to be safe."

Kit gasped and spun around. "Lola loves me."

"She does." Tack grinned proudly, and tucked Kit back under his arm. "He goes for a swim with her twice a week."

Dover shivered and hugged Chubber tighter. "In the cold water?"

Kit rolled his eyes. "It's not so bad, irmãozinho. Is everyone bundled up?" He pulled his fox-eared winter hat on and buttoned his coat over his baby bump. It barely fit. "Starfish shit, I'm going to need another coat."

"Petra already ordered you one." Tack helped him maneuver Blueberry into his coat pocket. The dragonling hadn't wanted to stay in their rooms, but he was sleepy after playing in the pool all morning.

Kit snuggled against Tack's side again as they led their group out of the castle.

Eugenia scowled. "No manacles hanging from the walls. No rats scurrying across the floor. Where's the starving peasants, Kit? Where?"

"Our nannies lied to us," Kit said, stifling his yawn. "All those tales they told about the Northern Silver Isles were wrong." *At least, nowadays, they are.*

"This place really is nice." Dover stroked a hand over one of the tapestries hanging on the wall. "I expected it to be cold and foreboding. No offense, Tack."

"Seriously." Eloise smiled and waved at a passing servant. "I haven't seen Tack or his father eat a single merbaby while we've been here. Eugenia said they ate babies."

Eugenia threw her hands in the air. "That's what I'm talking about! Where's the despair and horror?"

"Oh, the babies are on the menu for tonight," Kit said, grinning over his shoulder. "We served salmon and lobster last night to clear your palate."

Finch and a group of guards met them at the door. "Do you really have to go for a walk? Guarding you all takes up a lot of our time, you know."

Otis barked at him, so the Kelpie knelt down and pet the dog's sides.

Kit smiled. "I need more books."

Finch sighed. "I'll text Moxy. She's been on the lookout for more Italian vampires. She'll get what she has ready for you."

Dover clutched Chubber and moved closer to Kit. "That's a Kelpie," he whispered into Kit's ear.

"I know," Kit whispered back.

Finch bowed charmingly. "Prince Dover, it's a pleasure to meet you. I *am* a Kelpie, but I won't drown you."

"Damn right, you won't." Ben scowled. Rachael clucked from her spot under his arm.

Finch blinked and stared at the chicken, mouth opening and closing.

Tack nudged Ben with his shoulder. "You would probably jump into a lake of Kelpie, wouldn't you, human?"

Ben tapped his chin. "If my bluetail was in it, then yes, I would jump into a lake of Kelpie."

Finch grinned. "This is the human you told me about, isn't it? The one that jumped into shark infested waters with a dog and a beaver."

Tack laughed. "This would be him."

Kai snorted. "A few scraggly northern sharks aren't very frightening."

Tack smiled sharply over his shoulder. "Should we go for a swim?"

Eloise gave them a stern look and shook her finger. "Children, you had best behave, or I'll have to spank you."

Finch's eyes widened in delight. "Oh, please, please, please spank them."

Talia chuckled. "I think I'd pay to see that."

Kit rolled his eyes and tuned out their friendly teasing. Blueberry was a warm weight in his pocket, and his mate's arm was tight around his shoulders.

He had only been to town once before because he spent most of his time either in the castle or swimming with Lola.

Coalswell Tides was a harbor town with brightly colored houses and narrow, cobbled streets. The forest lined road leading from the castle to the town was a little slick from the icy rain, but the trees were beautiful with their red, gold, and orange leaves.

"Why are we walking to town and not driving?" Eugenia asked, pushing in between Kit and Dover.

Kit smiled and pointed at the trees. "That's why. Aren't they lovely?"

Eugenia shrugged. "They're trees and it's cold."

A familiar tiny figure flew down from a branch. "Hey, Hazelnut. Out visiting your old haunts today?"

The fairy tweeted something unintelligible and settled on his head. She rolled around on his hat and peeked around one of his fox ears.

Eugenia's eyes softened. "Okay, I can see why you like it so well here."

They spent the afternoon touring the town, shopping, and drinking in the pub. Kit spent far too much time in Moxy's bookstore.

The purple-haired merwoman handed Tack another stack of books. "This is a mix of Italian, French, and Spanish. They're all kinky as hell, so I knew you would like them."

Dover grinned. "Mother would make such a fuss if she saw your reading selection, Kit."

Eugenia waved a romance book in the air. "Mother can stuff it." She added it to the stack in Tack's arms. "That one's for me. I need some *Victorian lord meets beautiful peasant girl* love in my life."

Moxy came back with another stack. She looked around, then handed Kai the books. "These are for Pearl. I know she likes the cat books. They remind her of Chichi."

Chubber chirped loudly from atop a bookshelf. He waved a book in the air, then tossed it toward Kai.

Finch caught it before it hit Kai in the face. He settled it on top of Kai's stack of books. "I think the otter wants this one."

Kai gave Chubber a dry look. "Is that all?"

Chubber squealed, then grabbed one more and tossed it down.

Moxy's eyes bounced between them. "Does the chicken need a book too?"

By the time they left the town, Kit was almost asleep on his feet. Tack's arms were full of bags, so Kit couldn't move in for a snuggle and it was making him just a bit grumpy.

A hand on his shoulder made him growl.

Kai growled back, then laughed. "Come talk to me." He tugged Kit with him to the front of the group.

Kit wrapped his arms around his brother's waist, and they put more distance between them and the others. "I've missed you."

Kai settled his head on Kit's. "I've missed you too. I hate to admit it, but you fit in really well here. The damn Coalswells are taking good care of you and Pearl."

"They are." Kit's smile faded. "Kai, I don't think I'm a very good person."

Kai snorted. "Yeah, I'm pretty sure you're wrong about that."

"I don't want Tack to break his family curse."

Kai leaned back and gave him a surprised look. "What? Why not?"

"If he broke the curse, it means he met his mate. I know as soon as he meets them, they'll fall in love with him. I can't imagine why they wouldn't." Kit buried his face against his brother's shoulder. "I don't want Tack to be with anyone else, though. I know he deserves a true mate, but I want him for myself."

"You really like him."

"Yeah." Kit sniffed. "He's such a large part of what makes me happy. I can talk to him about anything, and he tells me things, too, important things. He respects me and asks for my opinion. He actually thinks I'm smart and beautiful."

"You *are* smart and beautiful." Kai scowled.

A slow smile crept across Kit's face. "I am, aren't I? They like my loudness here, Kai. I can just be me."

Kai groaned. "Fuck. I'm going to have to like the Coalswells now."

Kit chuckled. "Yes." He scrunched his nose. "Do you think I'm a bad person for wanting to keep Tack for myself?"

Kai gently shook him. "No, I think you're a merman who's found his treasure and doesn't want to share it."

They walked in silence for a moment. Kit could feel Hazelnut asleep on his head. Blueberry still sat in his pocket, but his head poked out. The dragonling was awake now and watched the woods with interest.

"Maybe, I can try to help one of the other Muirs break the curse," Kit whispered. "Then, Tack wouldn't suffer, but he would still be mine."

CHAPTER 18

*T*wo months later, Kit held onto Lola's fin as she pulled him through the lower castle. He had gotten to the point in his pregnancy where he didn't want to move. He remembered it well from his pregnancy with Pearl.

Below him, Grace and Jamie swam with Pearl. His daughter carried Blueberry in her arms, and the little dragonling looked happy.

Since Tack was processing the second load his cousin had sent him from the shipwreck, five guards swam around them. Kit personally thought his husband was a little too paranoid. There was no way Ailig and his pirates would try anything within the castle. The longer the search for Ailig and Eades went on, the more overprotective Tack became.

A large hammerhead appeared beside them and Kit peeked over Lola.

Finbar waved from the hammerhead's other side. "You've met Sara, haven't you?"

Kit nodded. "Her and Hugo swim with Lola and me sometimes."

"I don't spend enough time with her." Finbar patted his companion's side. "Tack wanted me to make sure you don't linger in the cold."

The water *was* much colder now that they were on the verge of winter. A month ago, it began snowing, and it had yet to stop. The bare limbs of the trees in the forest were covered with white, and the roads icy. Even Hazelnut was feeling the cold. She had demanded more blankets and stayed in her fairy house most of the time now.

"I miss Lola," Kit admitted. "I much prefer swimming in my pool, but Lola can't go there."

"Short swims won't hurt." Finbar traced his fingers over the carvings on the wall as they swam past. "This is nice. I never take the time to just swim."

"You're busy doing important stuff." Kit knew Finbar handled a lot of the export business for the kingdom. "You should take breaks sometime, though. Tack always makes time for a swim, but you and Nerio are workaholics."

Finbar gave him a sly look. "Tack has the incentive to take a break."

Kit flushed. "Good point." He gave Finbar a curious look. "Fin, have you heard the mating call?" Finbar paled and Kit immediately felt horrible for asking. "You don't have to answer that. I'm sorry."

Finbar's laugh was shaky. "It's been a long time since I spoke of it. Everyone knows what happened, so I've never had to explain it."

"Is it Petra?" Kit held his breath. He thought they'd make a great couple.

The other man's laugh was bitter. "Goddess, I wish it had been."

"You don't have to tell me."

Finbar shook his head. "It's alright, Kit. It hurts to remember, but I remember every day. Before the twins were born, I found my mate. She was the daughter of the Laird of Crossdows Cove."

"What did you decide to do?" Kit thought about Abernathy's own story. It seemed like the Muir family never made the right decision when they heard the mating call.

"I spoke with her father and arranged a marriage. I thought that perhaps if I had time with her, I could make her fall in love with me. I visited her often and showered her with gifts. I bought her the most expensive jewelry and finest clothing I could find. I did everything I could to impress her. Everything except for the most important thing."

Kit hugged Lola's fin. "What didn't you do?"

Finbar turned his head away. "I didn't listen to her. I spoke to her, not with her. I was arrogant and so sure no woman could resist falling for my wealth."

Kit awkwardly rolled over Lola's other side, then launched himself onto Sara so he could hug Finbar. "I'm sorry, Fin. What happened?"

"If I had made even a minor effort to learn something about her before forcing her into marriage, I would have known that Victoria was already in love with another laird. Her father was the one that wanted my wealth. He forced her to agree to the marriage even though it destroyed her to betray the man she loved."

Kit squeezed Finbar's shoulder, hating the agonized look on his face.

"A few weeks after our wedding, we visited Crossdows Cove. Dad and Tack came along so Tack could see the eastern coast. It's mostly cliffs and rocks, but it has its own beauty. Tack was only a few years old at the time." Finbar looked away. "Victoria said she wanted to spend some time alone with her father, so I went with Dad and Tack to the seashore. We had to climb down to it, but we were having fun collecting shells."

Kit looked down and watched Pearl with sad eyes. "What happened?"

"About an hour later, Victoria jumped off of the cliff above us and landed right beside Tack and I."

Kit opened his mouth to speak, but couldn't find the words.

"While we were gone, she killed her father, then made her way to the cliffs and jumped." Finbar's voice sounded hollow. "Afterwards, when everything was over and done, one of the servants told me about the other man – the one Victoria loved."

"Fin." Kit couldn't think of anything else to say.

Finbar rested his face against his arm and hugged Sara's fin. "There's a reason we haven't broken the damn curse yet. It seems like we're either monsters or fools. There's no in-between."

"That can't be true." Kit shook his head. "Father said that the curse guided him to act a certain way. Maybe the Muir curse did the same with you."

Finbar snorted. "I was a twenty-two-year-old wealthy prince with a high opinion of himself. The curse didn't make me that way. I did."

Kit's shoulders slumped. "Is there any hope of breaking it?"

The other man shrugged. "Father never pursued a mate, but I know Nerio has sensed his. I have my suspicions, but I don't think he'll pursue her. My experience scarred everyone."

Kit huffed. "What about Seamus and Hali?"

"Hali's a wild spirit." Finbar smiled softly. "I don't think she's met her mate, but it's hard to read her sometimes. Shay, on the other hand, wears his heart on his sleeve. He's met his mate and won't consider trying to win him over."

Kit bit his lip but refused to ask about Tack. He didn't want to know that Tack had already met his mate, but refused to do anything about it because of what happened between Fin and Victoria.

"You Muirs are a complicated lot."

WHILE PEARL TOOK AN AFTERNOON NAP, KIT AND TACK took advantage of the privacy.

Kit bunched the blanket in his fists, knees shaking. He tried to keep his cries quiet while Tack pushed a large dildo in and out of his ass, but Tack angled the toy and hit his prostate with each push.

His husband stroked a hand up and down his spine for a moment, then sped up the movement of the dildo again.

Kit groaned low. "Coming, coming, coming." He shot all over the blankets and his knees gave out.

Tack caught him up and lowered him down, away from the wet spot. He slid the dildo from Kit's ass and tossed it aside.

Kit barely paid attention. He had a full belly, a warm blanket, and had just come hard enough to see stars. "Nap time."

Tack chuckled. "Let's get cleaned up first, sweetling."

Kit's eyes popped open. "Oops, I'm sorry, tesoro mio. Let me take care of you."

Tack stroked his back again. "Too late. I came all over the blankets. Let's take a shower, and then you can take a nap."

He helped Kit out of bed and started the shower for him. While Kit scrubbed the sweat and cum away, Tack washed himself off at the sink.

I wish we could shower together. I wish I could kiss his bare lips. Kit pushed the thoughts away. All they did was cause pain.

Tack helped him dry off and dress, and Kit wished, not for the first time, that he could bend over.

"One day, I won't have this huge belly and I'll be able to see my feet again."

Tack smoothed a hand over the thick wool wrap covering Kit's stomach. "I like the belly. You're growing our child in there. He shivered. "It's a wonderful sight."

Kit felt shivery himself at the heat in Tack's eyes. It was so much nicer having a partner with him during this pregnancy. "Are you going to finish the article this afternoon?"

Tack made a face. "If I have to."

Kit laughed. "You said you loved writing for the archeology journal."

"That's when I don't have a sexy omega to cuddle with."

Kit pushed him out the door. "Go work!"

Tack groaned. "If you insist."

Kit shook his head and mumbled to himself. "Silly man." He pulled the dirty blanket from the bed and shoved it in the laundry hamper. The castle staff probably hated him.

He went to the kitchen and got a snack, smiling when Tack wiggled his eyebrows from the couch. "Keep working!"

Tack groaned but did as he was told.

Kit went back to his room and set a thimble full of apple cider on Hazelnut's porch. He knocked on her door with his pinky.

The fairy stuck her head out of the door and trilled.

"Hazelnut, here's your nightcap. I'll see you in the morning, alright?" He leaned closer and whispered. "Tack and I are going to mess around later tonight, so you may want to turn your music box on."

Hazelnut shook her head and sighed before grabbing the apple cider and slamming the door.

Kit looked at Blueberry. "Do you think she wants me to move her house? Tack and I, uh, cuddle a lot at night."

The dragonling was curled up on his favorite chair in the corner of the room. With plenty of food and love, the dragonling had grown quickly. He was still a baby, but he wasn't the tiny, squirrel-sized dragonling that Tack had brought him. Now he was almost as big as Chubber.

Blueberry lifted his head and huffed.

"Well, that answers that. I'll move her house later." Kit settled into his window seat and picked up his phone. He pulled up a baby name site. "Time to name this damn baby."

Seth, John, Will, Douglas, Harold, Marcus, Joseph... No, no, no.

An hour later, he still hadn't found a name he liked and Blueberry was curled against his side. "Why is this so hard?"

Pearl and Chichi came through the open door. "Daddy, does Chichi look pretty?"

The large cat wore a rabbit costume, ears and all. He didn't look pleased.

Kit grinned. "He's gorgeous, ma petite."

Pearl giggled and clapped, then ran back out of the room. "Otter Daddy, I'm hungry."

Kit winced. Fortunately, Tack had the patience of a saint and didn't seem to mind when Pearl interrupted his work.

Chichi's low growl drew his attention. Kit settled his hands on his belly and leaned back against the pillows. "You're the one that lets her dress you up, Chichi. It's your own fault."

The cat turned and stalked from the room, tail high in the air.

Kit picked his phone up and went back to the baby name site. "Nathan?" Kit wrinkled his nose. "That doesn't sound right."

Another hour passed and he still had no favorites. "Blueberry, you were easier to name than this damn kid."

"Are you still thinking about names?" Tack leaned against the door frame.

"I thought you were working?" Kit smiled and patted the spot beside him and Blueberry.

"I finished the article." Tack settled his large frame beside Kit. "I'll need to survey the actual wreckage again before I feel good about submitting it."

Kit entwined his fingers with Tack's. "Archeology journals are so hot."

Tack snorted. "Really? Do citations do it for you?"

Kit growled and tried to make a sexy face. "You know they do."

Tack's shoulders shook with his laughter. "I need to tell Hali you said that. She got her degree in archeology too, you know. She's enjoying the hell out the excavation."

Kit winced. "Do you miss it? For the most part, you've stayed right by my side since I arrived. I would understand if you wanted to get back to the Día Precioso."

Tack gave him a soft smile. "I'm right where I want to be."

Kit leaned his head on Tack's shoulder. *Fuck the curse. I'm never giving him up.*

CHAPTER 19

"*A*re you sure you want to go for a walk?" Seamus gave him a doubtful look. "You look like you're about to give birth and I've never delivered a baby before."

"None of us have." Luca frowned. "Winter isn't the best time for a walk, Prince Kit."

"We should have a least waited for more guards to come along," Anabelle said from behind him. "Two guards are a lot less than the five Prince Tack ordered on you at all times."

"If I don't get out of the castle, I'm going to murder someone," Kit said, smiling sweetly. "Do you want it to be you?"

Carina snorted. "And everyone calls you sweet."

Tack was meeting Hali at the harbor today, and Kit was driving himself mad worrying over meeting Tack's cousin. She was the only family member he hadn't met, and he was afraid she wouldn't like him.

"Daddy is grumpy today." Pearl skipped beside him,

Blueberry in her arms. Chichi ran through the snow beside them. This time, the cat was dressed as a bumblebee. The Norwegian Forest cat jumped from snow pile to snow pile, a blur of yellow and black.

"Daddy *is* grumpy, ma petite." Kit rubbed his belly. The quiet peacefulness of the woods along the road calmed him. "Moxy has some books for me, and that will make me happy again."

Pearl grabbed Luca's hand and dragged him ahead. "I like Moxy."

"You could have sent me to get them," Carina said, sighing.

Kit glared at her. "Don't you sigh at me."

"Prince Grumpy." Carina rolled her eyes and fell behind to walk with Anabelle.

Seamus linked his arm with Kit's. "Okay, what's really wrong?"

Kit tried to look unconcerned, but he broke under Seamus's stare. "What if Hali doesn't like me?"

"Then she won't talk to you, and you'll be a lucky man."

"Seriously, Shay. What if she realizes I'm a big, awkward idiot, and the rest of you finally see it?"

Seamus chuckled. "Too late. I was there when you and Laird Sutton pranked Uncle Nerio with hot sauce in his coffee. The way you waddled away, giggling, was hilarious. I know you're a big, awkward idiot, but I also know how loving and kind you are. Hali's not dumb. She'll see it too."

"Nerio has been acting funny." Kit rubbed his cheeks with his hands. "I keep seeing him stare out the window sadly. It's like he's one of those princesses locked in a tower while she waits for her prince to come."

"Okay, maybe you do read too many romance books."

"That's a fairy tale. Completely different thing."

Seamus looked behind him at Anabelle and Carina, then leaned closer. "I think Uncle Nerio knows who his mate is."

"Why doesn't he go after her?"

"Her?" Seamus narrowed his eyes.

"Your dad thinks he knows who it is." Kit shrugged. "I don't know."

Seamus shook his head. "In any case, it's never wise for a Muir to pursue their mate. We all learned that lesson."

Kit groaned, frustrated at their stubbornness. "What about you, Seamus? Your dad thinks you've met your mate too."

Seamus shook his head. "There's no way it could work. In my case, if I stay out of it, my mates can just meet and fall in love with one another with no reason to worry about my curse."

Kit pulled him to a stop. "Mates? As in plural?"

Seamus nodded, cheeks pinkening. "They're both so handsome, Kit. Even if I wasn't cursed, there's no way either of them would want to be with me."

Kit frowned and looked Seamus over. The seal tailed mer was short, with dark brown hair and eyes. He was a little chunky but carried it well. His round face was sweet, and he liked to smile. "I don't understand. You're lovely."

Seamus rolled his eyes. "Well, you aren't one of my mates, so it doesn't matter. Trust me. It won't work."

Kit sighed. "You Muir men make me want to shake you until you see reason."

Seamus laughed. "You sound like Grandpa's bestie. Laird Riverpine gets so mad at him when he won't do something. Before his wife died, she would give Grandpa hell too."

Kit's eyes widened, and he pulled Seamus to a stop. "Laird Riverpine? Cyreus, the laird of Riverpine Coast?"

Seamus looked bemused. "Yes? I didn't think you had met him. He usually waits until spring to come and visit Grandpa."

"His wife is dead?"

Seamus tilted his head. "Yes, and she was a really nice woman, so why do you look so happy?"

Kit winced. "I'm not happy she's dead. I'm happy Cyreus isn't married anymore."

"Well, you are married, so his status shouldn't matter." Seamus wrinkled his nose. "He's as old as Grandpa. Why would you want him anyway?"

Kit sniffed. "Age is just a number, but I don't want him for me." He narrowed his eyes. "You Muir men really, really piss me off sometimes."

Pearl's scream sent ice down his back.

Kit looked ahead. A dozen strangers with guns and knives stood in front of Luca and Pearl.

"Pearl," he whispered, eyes watering.

Luca acted fast and picked Pearl up, tossing her into the wooded trees, while Chichi launched himself at one of the strangers' faces.

The others were on Luca in a flash.

Anabelle pushed Kit and Seamus behind her. "Carina, get them back to the castle as soon as you can."

She raised her gun and fired into the mass of bodies around Luca as she ran.

As one, they ran to the woods. Kit found Pearl in a snowdrift with Blueberry. "Daddy, is my Luca and Chichi okay?"

"They'll be fine, ma petite. We need to get to the castle."

Carina picked her up and balanced Pearl on her hip. Blueberry chirped, but Pearl had a good hold on the dragonling.

They turned and ran toward the castle, but it was slow going since Kit couldn't run very fast.

"I'll get him," Seamus said, grabbing his arm. "Get Pearl to safety."

Carina looked torn. "Okay. Hurry. I don't think Luca and Anabelle can hold them off much longer."

She ran ahead, Pearl bouncing on her hip.

Seamus pulled him toward the castle, and Kit forced himself to move faster.

He saw Carina and Pearl disappear around a bend in the road, then felt a blow to the side of his head. He blinked, falling into Seamus's arms.

His friend grabbed him, holding him tight as two men moved in front of them. The one on the left watched Seamus with hate-filled blue eyes. "Looks like we get one of Finbar's brats too. Lucky us." He nodded to the man beside him. "Go get the girl too."

"No," Kit whispered, voice hoarse. "Please, no."

"Yes, sir." The man ran after Carina and Pearl. He didn't get far.

Kit recognized Hazelnut, even from a distance. His fairy friend flew at the head of a swarm of fairies armed with long, sharp thorns as spears.

Hazelnut screeched and stabbed at the man with her thorn. The fairies surrounded him, and he was soon lost to Kit's sight behind the swarm.

Kit winced at the man's screams.

The blue eyed stranger snarled and waved his gun. "Forget the girl. Move it."

"We aren't going anywhere with you," Seamus said, holding Kit closer to him.

Kit heard ice crunch behind him and felt the blow to his head. Everything disappeared in a haze of pain.

CHAPTER 20

*S*eamus's tear-filled voice woke him up. "Kit, please wake up. I swear to the Goddess, if you die, I'll never forgive you."

His eyes fluttered open, and he winced at the light filtering into the large, underwater cavern. His head ached horribly.

"Kit?" Seamus looked down at him. They were both in their merform, and the water was freezing. His large bulky coat was meant for land and offered no warmth.

"What happened?" He whispered. It looked like they were in a cell.

"Three men grabbed us. They knocked you unconscious and told me they would kill you if I tried to run." Seamus shivered. "I saw Luca and Ana on the ground. I don't know if they made it. I couldn't see Chichi at all."

Kit whimpered and closed his eyes. *Goddess, please let them all be okay. I shouldn't have been so selfish and impatient.*

"Pearl and Carina got away. I heard them complaining about it." Seamus pulled him closer and settled Kit's head on his stomach. "The three men brought us to a helicopter, then flew us to the eastern coast. They kept me blindfolded after that. It's been hours, Kit. I thought you would die."

"The baby?"

Seamus sniffed and wiped his eyes. "I don't know, but I felt him kick an hour ago."

Kit breathed out slowly. "Okay. That's something."

A young voice came from the shadows. "He okay?"

Seamus smiled. "I think he will be. You can come back out, Oscar. He won't bite."

A very young tentacle-tailed merboy swam into the light. He looked to be about six and was far too skinny for his age. His tentacles were a smooth black with dark purple undersides, and he had soft violet hair and very pale skin.

Kit frowned. There was an iron collar around his neck. It bit into this skin and was hooked to a chain.

"He's chained to the wall," Seamus whispered, voice shaking with anger.

Oscar swam as close as he could. "They never bring anyone down here. They all live in the caverns above."

"Why are you here, Oscar?" Kit asked, keeping his voice soft. "Where are your parents?"

Oscar shrugged. "My parents follow Ailig."

"Why would they chain you up down here?" Kit rubbed his forehead, unable to fathom how the boy's parents could put a collar around his neck and chain him to the wall."

Oscar bit his lip and retreated toward the shadows.

"May I tell him what you told me, Oscar?" Seamus asked.

The boy's voice floated from the dark. "Okay."

"His parents were from the Southern Silver Isles and are idiots that didn't like his tentacle tail," Seamus said, voice hard. "They kept him around, though, instead of abandoning him to the Deep. When he was about Pearl's age, his tail turned black."

Oscar whimpered.

Seamus gave Kit a pained look. "They started hurting him, but he learned a trick. He could hide from everyone while he was in the water."

"Ailig found out," Oscar whispered. "He chained me up. If I want food, I have to hide the camp. The water likes me, so if I ask nicely, it hides the caverns."

"I'm so sorry, Oscar." Kit swallowed hard and sat up. "When my husband comes, he'll make sure you get out of here."

A taunting voice came from the cavern entrance. "When your husband comes? No one will find us here."

The blue eyed merman from the castle swam forward. His orca tail carried him through the water quickly. He looked to be in his late forties or early fifties and was well built and clearly a fighter. He carried a harpoon gun and several blades.

"Ailig," Oscar whispered.

"You aren't going to make it home, prince." Ailig's smile was full of malice. "I can't say I'm sorry. I've heard Finbar and the rest of the family is fond of you."

His eyes darkened with rage when they fell on Seamus. "You, oh, I will enjoy killing you."

"What the hell did we do to you?" Kit asked, angry. "Why are you doing this? It won't bring you the throne. Everyone in the Northern Silver Isles will die before bowing to you."

Ailig grinned. "I don't want the throne. I want the whole Muir family to suffer as I suffered all these years. My beloved Victoria didn't deserve to be chained to one of the Muir monsters. Finbar drove her to kill herself." He gripped the bars and snarled. "I'll take everything of his until he can't bear to live. Then I'll cut his fucking head from his body."

"You're the man she loved." Kit shook his head. "Ailig, this won't bring you peace or bring Victoria back. It was a tragedy, but Finbar didn't kill her."

The man shook the bars and growled. "Don't you say her name, filth!"

Kit resisted shrinking back. "Do you know what killed her, Ailig?"

Ailig's face darkened, and his eyes glowed with hate.

Kit kept his eyes fixed on Ailig. "Victoria killed herself. If she didn't want to marry Finbar, she should have refused."

"Her father wouldn't let her," Ailig roared and shook the bars again. "He forced her to go through with it."

"Then why not run away with you?" Seamus asked quietly.

Ailig paled.

"Oh," Kit said softly, understanding. "You didn't offer."

"I was a laird. I had responsibilities." His voice grew louder with each word.

"Ailig, calm down." Kit recognized Eades when the man came into the light. He looked a little rougher, but his sneer was still the same. "Save all that energy for the battle ahead. We have plans for these two, and look what my darling brought us."

Two pirates pulled Queen Kelby into the room.

"Mother." Kit moved to the bars, but Seamus pulled him back.

Kelby struggled between them. "Let me go, you miscreants."

Another well-armed pirate carried a large chest into the room and set it in the corner. For the first time, Kit noticed a pile of very familiar looking treasure.

Ailig smiled slowly. "That should get King Ren's attention. How did you manage to snag her?"

A familiar voice came from the dark. "She followed me from the treasury, and your men grabbed her." Lorelei swam deeper into the room, a spiteful smile on her face. "Ailig, you would have loved seeing Father yell at the northern king. Everyone's in a panic because those two are missing."

Ailig sneered. "Good."

Eades pulled Lorelei to him. "You're an angel, princess." He bent and kissed her, his parrotfish tail twisting to wrap around her angelfish tail.

"Eww." Kit wrinkled his nose. "I should have known

Lorelei would betray her family. Is this supposed to somehow put you on a throne?"

The door to the cell opened, and the two pirates pushed Kelby into the room. She swam to Kit and pulled him into her arms.

Lorelei and Eades broke their kiss, and his sister smirked. "Eades promised to make me his queen. His wife and son left him for the Pacific months ago. The fools thought he was wasting his time. Now, with you three to use for leverage, it'll be easy enough to manipulate Father and King Nerio. Then, when all the dust settles, Ailig gets the north to do with what he wants, and we'll run the south." She turned to Ailig. "I brought more money since the Morey family stopped backing us. We need to hire more mercenaries. I know they won't find us here, but we should be prepared just in case."

Ailig growled. "Let's send the fat seal's head to Finbar tonight. I want to see his face when he knows his son is dead."

Eades rolled his eyes. "Not yet. Ailig, you must think long term. I know you want to hurt Prince Finbar, but be patient. Wouldn't you rather his whole kingdom crumble around him?"

Ailig licked his teeth, then swam for the door. "Whatever."

Eades gave him an annoyed look, then took Lorelei's arm. "Come with me, my dear. I'll show you the rest of the caverns. They aren't much, but we'll be sitting in Latch Bay Castle soon enough."

Kit waited for them all to leave before turning to his mother. "What happened?"

"Exactly what Lorelei said. I got curious and followed her. Those goons grabbed me." Kelby sighed. "Ren is furious with Nerio. He trusted him to keep you safe while we dealt with the pirates. Fergus, oh my poor Fergus, is heartbroken. He went straight to Kai and Talia. They're gathering our soldiers now."

"To do what?" Kit asked, worried.

Kelby smiled slyly and leaned in to whisper in his ear. "To bring them here."

Kit gasped. "Lorelei?"

"She's wearing a tracker." Kelby smoothed a hand over his belly. "You're alright?"

"I think so. Seamus felt the baby kick earlier." Kit smiled when he saw Seamus floating beside Oscar. "Mother, this is Oscar. We'll need to find him a home when we're rescued."

"No, you don't." Seamus wrapped an arm around Oscar's bony shoulders. "He's my son now. I'll bring him home and cook him all the food he wants. We'll swim in your pool and play with Betty and Veronica all day long. Pearl could use a cousin to play with, don't you think?"

Oscar stared at Seamus, eyes full of adoration. "Really?"

Seamus nodded sharply. "Really."

"Well, never mind then." Kit hid his smile. "Pearl will be happy for a new cousin."

"Kit." Kelby turned him to face her. "I'm so sorry."

"For what?"

"For everything." She sniffed. "Your fathers lectured me when we got home from our *visit*. Then Shauna and Dover came and gave me a talking to. A day later, Petra called me. She was very hateful and listed out everything I did wrong. Even that Otter, Shell, cornered me in the castle and yelled at me. At least I think she was yelling. She acted very angry."

Kit blinked. "An otter yelled at you?"

"Yes." Kelby scowled. "Apparently, she's a better mother than me."

Kit hugged her. "A year ago, I never would have dreamed of hugging you. You've always been so critical, Mother. I just wanted to be me, but it seemed like that was never the right thing to do."

Kelby gasped and hugged him tight. "I love you, Kit. You're a beautiful person, I swear. I only ever wanted life to be easier for you. That's why I kept trying to get you to act like everyone else. Seeing you happy and loved in Coalswell Tides made me so angry. I wanted you to be happy with me."

He scrunched his nose. "I don't know what to say."

"You don't have to say anything." Kelby kissed his cheek. "I'll try to do better, but please be patient with me, and don't hesitate to yell at me. I've noticed it gets results."

Kit's laugh was a little ragged. He pulled Kelby over to Oscar's other side, and they floated beside him. "Now, we just wait for Tack to come get us."

His thoughts swirled. *My mother apologized, and she wants to be a better person.* Kit closed his eyes and pictured his husband's sweet half-smile and heated dark eyes. He wanted his warm arms around him. *A better person would put the one they love above all else. I love Tack. I. Love. Tack.* He opened his eyes, heart beating hard in his chest. *I love him enough to let him go. He deserves to find his mate and break the curse. He deserves to be happy.*

He hugged his belly as his tears mixed with the sea.

CHAPTER 21

*T*ack paced the floors in his father's study, Pearl held tight in his arms. His little girl was asleep, finally, her head settled on his chest.

Hazelnut buzzed around his head, crying. The fairy and her friends had killed a man to protect Pearl and Kit, but now she was as big a mess as Tack.

Tack glanced at his dad's desk. Chichi slept on a pillow next to Nerio. Blueberry curled around him. The cat had refused to stay in their rooms, even though he was still drowsy from his surgery. He had a few new scars but would recover.

Luca and Anabelle, on the other hand, weren't so lucky. Both were still in critical care, and the doctors said it was too early to know if they would live or die. The two had held their ground so Kit and the others could escape, but they had been outnumbered.

"Ren, I swear to the Goddess, we will get them back," Nerio spoke into the phone. "We're readying our soldiers now. As soon as you have the location, we'll move."

Hali sat with Finbar and Abernathy. His cousin picked at her nails, face full of worry. "It's been hours, and we haven't gotten a call."

"They won't just kill them." Finbar shook his head. "If that was the plan, Ailig wouldn't have bothered taking them with him."

"How the fuck did they get a helicopter into Coalswell Tides?" Abernathy scowled. "That's hard to miss."

"Laird Dougal helped them." Finch leaned against the wall near the door. "My guards are questioning him, but it looks like he doesn't know much. Ailig offered him a lot of money to give him clearance to get past our air control."

"You have the location?" Nerio waved his hands to get their attention. "Tell me, Ren, and we'll bring an army."

Tack's body shook, so he settled Pearl down into the window seat next to Carina. The guppy tail gave him a sad smile. "I'll watch over her, Prince Tack."

He nodded, words stuck in his throat.

Nerio looked up, face pale. "Crossdows Cove."

Finbar's sunken eyes flashed. "Of course, that's where the fucker would set up his base."

Abernathy grabbed his phone. "Cy's lands are near there, and he wants to help. We can bring our soldiers to his estate and launch the attack from there."

"Ren, I'll give you coordinates to bring your own

soldiers by air," Nerio said. "We go in together and take them out."

Tack smoothed a finger down Pearl's plump cheek, and her eyes fluttered open. "Otter Daddy? Is Daddy and Unki Shay home yet?"

"Not yet, little bit. We're going to get them now." He plucked Hazelnut from the air above his head and set her next to Pearl. "Carina, Hazelnut, and Chichi are going to stay here with you. Get some rest, okay?"

Pearl nodded, eyes full of tears. "We go play with Tahli in pool."

"That sounds like fun," Carina said softly.

Tack felt a weight at his shoulder and scratched Blueberry's head. "You'll stay here too, Blue."

The dragonling hissed and dug his claws into Tack's shoulder.

"I'm thinking that was a no," Hali said dryly.

Tack shook his head. He didn't have the energy or willpower to argue with the dragonling. *I need my mate safe in my arms and my cousin safe in the damn castle.*

TACK HELD BLUEBERRY CLOSE AND JUMPED OFF THE helicopter. He ran toward the old Riverpine Manor. He had lost count of the number of times Abernathy had brought him here to visit as a child. He had quickly become good friends with Laird Riverpine's granddaughter, Mabel.

Mabel opened the door for him, Finch, and Hali.

"The others are already here. They've taken the southern queen too."

Tack froze. "Queen Kelby?"

"Yes." Mabel bit her lip. "Princess Talia said her mother was following their spy and got caught."

"Damn it." Tack rubbed his face. "This is turning into a nightmare."

Mabel patted his arm. "I'm so sorry this happened, Tack. We'll find Seamus and your husband."

Tack nodded but couldn't say anything. All he could think about was finding them. He went straight to Cyreus's study. King Ren and the rest of the southern merfolk were already there. They stood around a map of Crossdows Cove.

Kai met him half way, and Tack braced himself for the hit he knew was coming. He had failed to keep his promise to protect Kit.

He wasn't expecting the one arm hug Kai gave him as he steered him toward the group. "Our scouts are already back. The place is crawling with pirates and mercenaries. I wish your sharks could get here as quickly as you did."

"Me too." Tack studied the map. Crossdows Cove was a huge territory, but three small circles marked the water right off the coast. "Is that where they're at? Sea Witch Johanna said they couldn't be in the water because she couldn't sense them."

"She was wrong," Cyreus said. The old guppy tailed merman was a welcome presence. He had always been so calm and good-natured, which contrasted well with Abernathy's kookiness. "Off the coast, there is a line of underwater caverns. Aber and I explored them all the time when we were kids. They'd be the perfect hiding space for a group of pirates."

"Lorelei's tracker went straight here." Talia tapped one of the circles. "She must have gone in there."

"I suggest we attack at night," Kai said, arms crossed. "That gives us a few hours to get in place. We still have soldiers coming."

"We do too," Finch said, nodding. "Plus, we have night goggles, and from what I can tell, Ailig's pirates don't have the gear we do. They will be relying on any lighting they've rigged in the caverns."

Kai nodded. "True."

Abernathy studied the map and pointed to three spots around the red circle. "If I'm remembering right, these are the three cavern entrances."

Tack took a breath and released it. "If we join our soldiers together, we can split into three large groups and invade these points."

"We push in, and we find them," Ren said softly, eyes glittering. "Fergus and I will take this entrance." He tapped the one farthest north. "It's been a while since we fought, but we can still hold our own. Cyreus, can you come with us? If you're familiar with the layout of the caverns, that would be helpful."

Cyreus gave Ren a brief bow. "I'd be happy too. Mabel can help one of the other groups."

"Kai and I can take this one." Talia pointed at the middle entrance. "Mabel, will you come?"

Mabel nodded from the door. "Sure thing, your

highness. I haven't been there in years, but I spent enough time in them to remember my way around."

"Finch and I will take the last entrance. Dad can help us navigate the caverns," Nerio asked.

Abernathy scowled. "Try to stop me."

Nerio patted Tack's shoulder. "You and Finbar focus on finding Seamus, Kit, and Queen Kelby."

Tack nodded and patted Blueberry's head. "I brought our own trackers. We'll find them quickly."

Ben moved from his seat in the corner. "Hopefully, we'll have numbers on our side. I would suggest leaving some reinforcement units outside. Also, Laird Riverpine is lending us as many boats as he can get quickly. I'll have medics waiting above for any wounded."

Ren gave the human a fond look. "Thank you, Ben. I think those are good ideas."

Ben shrugged. "I wish I could go with you."

Tack tuned the rest of the conversation out and started checking his weapons. He planned on putting a harpoon through Ailig's forehead.

CHAPTER 22

*K*elby wiggled the tip of her jeweled hairpin in the heavy lock on Oscar's collar. "I almost have it, darling. Try to stay still."

"How do you even know how to pick locks, Mother?" Kit asked, amazed. He floated, arm in arm, with Seamus as Kelby worked her magic.

"My parents were far stricter than I am, Kit. You should be thankful you never had to break out of your room to go to a heat swarm."

Kit gasped, unable to decide if he was impressed or grossed out. "You joined in a heat swarm?"

"A girl has needs. When you got pregnant with Pearl, I should have remembered how I felt then." Kelby bit her lip. "Almost, almost, almost. There!"

The collar popped off and fell to the ground with a thud.

Oscar grinned and swam to Seamus. He wrapped his tentacles around the seal-tail mer and hugged him.

"Be careful of the skin, Ozzy." Seamus hugged him back.

"I remember." Oscar's thin arms wrapped around his waist.

Kit pulled his mother to the locked door. "Work your magic again, delinquent."

Kelby giggled and set to work on the lock.

They heard movement at the entrance, and Seamus quickly pulled Oscar back into his shadows, dragging the chain and collar with him.

Kelby stuffed her pin into her hair.

Lorelei swam in, grinning. "The attack has begun. Eades is shitting himself. Thank the Goddess, I didn't have to sleep with him. Explaining how I wanted to save my virginity for marriage was getting tiring."

Kit snorted. "He believed you?"

She glared at him and swam to the door, brandishing a key. "I haven't let you out yet, Kit."

"Lorelei." Kelby gave her a hard look. "Hurry up, dear. We don't have time to argue."

Lorelei hurried and unlocked the cell, then ran over to the large chest of gold and gems she had given Ailig.

"We can get that later," Kelby said, guiding Kit from the cell.

Lorelei popped the lid on the chest and buried her hands in the treasure. "Give me just a second."

Seamus pulled Oscar behind him. The young boy had his tentacles wrapped around Seamus again and looked frightened. Kit wondered how long he had been in the cell.

"Yes!" Lorelei grinned and pulled a long knife from

the chest. "There are two in here. Hold on, and I'll get the other."

"Lorelei, we don't have time," Kelby said, arms tightening around Kit.

"Time for what?" Ailig asked from the entrance. A large number of pirates stood behind him. "Oh, I see. You're busy escaping."

Kelby grabbed the knife Lorelei had uncovered and shoved Kit behind her. "Please, just let us go."

"Hmm." Ailig tapped his chin. "What should I do?"

Lorelei pulled the second knife from the chest and moved to stand in front of Seamus and Oscar. Her arm shook as she held the blade up.

Seamus rolled his eyes and removed his gloves. He took the knife from her and shoved Lorelei and Oscar toward Kit and Kelby.

Ailig started laughing and waved to the guards behind them. "Kill the others. I want the fat seal."

Seamus darted forward, meeting the first guard head on. The man blocked his knife, but Seamus pressed his hand to the pirate's face. The man wailed in pain, body convulsing until he fell into unconsciousness.

The others paused, staring at the fallen merman.

"Go," Ailig snapped.

The pirates moved for Kelby and Kit.

"No!" Oscar held his hands up, and the water around the pirates swirled, pushing their attackers back toward the entrance.

Ailig growled and fired a harpoon toward them.

Lorelei pulled Oscar to the side just in time, but the boy's concentration broke.

Ailig snarled. "I should have killed you when your mother brought you to me, brat. Kill them," he ordered again.

Eades pushed through the guards. "Wait, wait. We need them so we can live through this, Ailig. We're outnumbered, and they've cut off all the exits. Ren and Nerio are *working together*. We don't stand a chance."

Ailig laughed and stabbed his spear toward Seamus. "I don't give a damn about living. Finbar will be crushed when his precious son is dead when he arrives to save him."

Seamus barely moved in time to avoid being skewered.

Eades cursed and swam to Kit and the others. "Fine, Ailig. Kill the Muir, but the others can be ransomed." He glared at Lorelei. "Except for the whore."

Kit scowled. "Don't call her that, asshole."

Eades grabbed Lorelei's arm. "I'll call her whatever –" Kelby's knife slid deep into his side. Eades looked down, surprised.

Kelby pulled her knife back, then slammed it into Eades again. "My family has had enough of you."

Seamus's cry of pain drew Kit's attention. Ailig pulled his spear tip from Seamus's shoulder.

"Shay," Oscar called out, voice thick with tears. He raised his hands again, and the water around Ailig swirled. Oscar moved his hands and churning water slammed Ailig into his pirates before gathering them all up and slinging them hard against the cavern wall.

Kit swam as fast as he could and pulled Seamus to the rest of the group. He studied the wound, then pressed hard against it to stifle the bleeding. "I don't think it was too deep."

"I'll be okay, Oscar," Seamus whispered. "I really wish I practiced more with Tack and Hali."

Oscar yelped when two dark blurs burst into the cavern, swimming straight to them. One of the blurs carried a familiar blue and white dragonling.

"That's Betty and Veronica." Seamus smiled. "What are you two doing here?"

The two harbor seals circled his group protectively.

"Blueberry." Kit sniffled and pulled his dragonling into a hug. "It's too dangerous for you to be here."

Eades struggled to grab Kelby's arm, eyes full of pain and rage. "Stupid bitch."

Blueberry growled, then launched himself at Eades's throat, quickly finishing the man off.

"I want a dragonling to kill my enemies," Lorelei pouted.

"Stuff it." Kit pulled Blueberry away from Eades's body and noticed Oscar's hands were shaking. "The door is blocked, and Oscar looks tired."

The boy panted, looking paler than before. "I can't hold them anymore."

Seamus pulled Oscar close and Betty booped the merboy's nose with her snout. "I have a feeling help is here."

Kit squeaked when he saw a familiar face. "Tack."

Finbar and Tack pushed into the room, and the guards turned their attention to them. Tack sent a harpoon through one pirate and cut into another with one of the many blades he carried.

Ailig growled and jabbed his spear toward Finbar. "You'll die, just like my Victoria."

"Damn it, Ailig. I don't want to kill you," Finbar said, voice full of agony. "I'd give anything to bring her back for you."

Ailig grinned and spun toward Kit and the others. "Would you give your son?" He drew back his arm, spear aimed for Seamus.

Finbar's blade cut into the back of Ailig's neck, severing his head.

Kit covered Oscar's eyes and watched Ailig's body floating listlessly in the water. *I've reached my limit. This is too much, damn it.*

"Dad, I'm so sorry." Seamus held out his good arm. "I know you didn't want to do that."

Finbar's eyes softened, then he turned to face the rest of the fight. "Seriously, Tack? There were nine guards, and you couldn't save me one?"

Tack winced when he pulled his spear from the last. "You were busy."

Blood filled the water around Tack, and Kit noticed the deep cut on his side. "Oh, Goddess, look what they've done to you, tesoro mio." He swam to Tack's side and curled into him, pressing the bottom of his coat against the deep wound. "You're bleeding."

"It's okay, sweetling. It's just a cut. It looks worse than it is."

Kit couldn't control the panicked spill of words. "They've killed you. I don't want you to die, Tack. I'm leaving you so you can find your mate, but you have to be alive to do that."

"I'm not dy... Wait, did you say you were leaving me?" Tack's eyes filled with pain. "I swear I'll protect you better, Kit. Please don't leave me."

"I have to, Tack. You deserve to find your mate and break the curse." Kit's voice broke, and he looked away. "I love you, Tack. I love you enough to let you go."

CHAPTER 23

*T*ack's heart stopped at Kit's words. *I love you, Tack.* The cold water, the dead bodies, and the people watching them suddenly didn't matter. He dropped his spear and knife and pulled his gloves off.

"Are you sure, Kit? You swear it?" he asked, voice rough.

Kit looked away. "I swear. I'll set you free, Tack."

Tack cupped Kit's cheeks, almost moaning at the soft silken skin and prickly stubble on Kit's chin. He pressed his lips to Kit's, shuddering at the taste of his mate. His tongue eased between Kit's lips, and Tack was lost.

He pulled Kit to him, his shark tail twisting with Kit's much shorter clownfish tail.

Kit groaned into his mouth, and his arms moved around Tack's neck. He ran his hands through Tack's hair, fingers gripping his head.

Tack had never felt so intoxicated and out of

control. *This must be what the heat swarm feels like.* All he wanted was to make Kit his.

Their tails rubbed together, and one of Tack's claspers slid into the small opening hidden in Kit's scales. It was tight, but he fit. The spur on Tack's clasper expanded inside of Kit, holding his clasper in place as it pulsed, sending waves of pleasure through him. They moved together, spinning in the water as their tails entwined.

Kit's mouth left his, and he cried out, body shuddering. He moved his head to the side, baring his neck for Tack. Tack bit down hard, feeling their mating bond slowly forming.

Kit's fingers dug into Tack's back as their tails thrashed roughly together. Tack's second clasper edged along Kit's stretched hole. Kit barely fit around his first clasper, so Tack pulled back, worried that two would be too much for Kit.

"Don't you dare," Kit hissed, fingers pulling Tack's hair. "I want all of you."

Tack released Kit's neck and watched his blood pinken the water. "Mate me?"

Kit didn't answer. Instead, his teeth latched onto Tack's neck, biting deep. Tack groaned and slowly began to push his second clasper into Kit's hole.

Kit whimpered around his bite, fingers digging into Tack's shoulders, but his tail tapped Tack's urging him on. Tack pushed forward, body shaking at the tightness surrounding him. He felt their mating bond snap into place as the spur on his second clasper expanded, locking them tightly together.

Kit released his neck, and the water turned pink again. "Goddess, help me." They spun faster, tails twisting and releasing as Tack's claspers pulsed.

He wasn't sure how long they stayed locked together, but he didn't really care. He had his mate, his sweetling, in his arms.

His first clasper pulsed one last time, filling Kit with his seed. Kit's body shook by the time Tack's second clasper released.

Kit buried his face against Tack's neck and panted.

Slowly, their tails pulled apart, and their spinning dance ended. Tack could feel Kit through their bond. He felt his satisfaction and exhaustion. He felt his love.

Kit's lips were swollen, and Tack couldn't resist touching them. "I've loved you for a long time, Kit. Finch and I snuck into Latch Bay one day, just to say we did it. You were seventeen at the time. I knew you existed, but we hadn't met. I saw you and Kai playing with Dover in the royal reefs. I knew right then that you were what pulled me to Latch Bay."

"Tack." Kit cupped his face and kissed him gently. "You're an idiot."

Tack pulled back. "What?"

Kit leaned up and nipped his chin. "Why the hell didn't you tell me we were mates? Do you know how long I've wanted someone of my own?"

"You wouldn't have wanted me." Tack pressed his forehead to Kit's. "To you, I was just one of the Coalswells. I'm still surprised your father let you marry me."

Kit's head snapped up, and his mouth dropped open. "Please tell me we didn't have sex in front of everyone."

"Fucking hell, I forgot we weren't alone." He looked around the empty cavern. "Okay, well, no one's here. Let's hope they left quickly."

Kit groaned and thumped his head against Tack's chest. "There was a child in the room. We're monsters."

"Are you two done yet?" Lorelei's voice filtered in from outside the entrance. "Two old guys are kissing out here, and you two are fucking in there. We're blocked in, damn it."

"Lorelei, watch your language," Kelby said.

"Two old guys?" Tack asked, head tilted.

Kit grabbed Tack's cheeks and smooshed his cheeks together. "The curse broke!"

"Yes," Tack said, through puffed up cheeks. "I was here, sweetling."

"That means Aber and Cy can finally be together." Kit pushed him away and swam for the entrance. "It better not be two *other* old guys kissing, or I'm cutting Lorelei's hair while she sleeps."

"What?" Tack asked. He winced when his side pulled. "I'm practically dying over here, remember?"

Kit rolled his eyes. "You were just fine when we were fucking."

Tack grumbled as he followed his mate from the cavern. Bodies littered the hallway, and the wounded were being tended to. Betty and Veronica helped other seal and dolphin companions carry the wounded to the surface, after medics from both kingdoms patched them up as well as they could underwater.

It was odd to see the northern and southern merfolk mixing.

That wasn't what drew his attention, however. Abernathy and Cyreus were kissing one another. "What the hell?"

Kelby winced. "One moment we were speaking with Abernathy and the next thing I know, this other man barreled into him and started yelling. Then they were kissing."

Tack saw their tails twist around each other and knew exactly what was about to happen. "Shit." He swam quickly to the men and shoved them into the empty cavern. "There are children present, Grandpa."

"Like that stopped you," Seamus said, grinning. A young tentacle tail merboy was wrapped around Seamus, cheek pressed to his. Finbar held them both, his bare hand stroking Seamus's forehead.

Lorelei smirked. "Don't worry, Prince Tack. We didn't see much."

"Really Kit, did you have to mate your husband right there in front of everyone?" Kelby propped her hands on her hips.

"I thought you said you didn't see much?" Kit asked, eyes narrowed.

Kelby flushed. "Well, we didn't, but I could see where it was going."

Tack rubbed his face. "We need to help the wounded and start counting casualties."

"The pirates are dead," Finbar said. "Ben's medics are pulling out the wounded now."

"Kelby," Fergus yelled.

Kit's fathers swam down the halls, soldiers following behind them.

"Darling," Ren said softly. He pulled Kit's mother into his arms. "You are never to follow one of our children when they're acting suspicious again."

Kelby kissed Ren's cheek. "I promise nothing. They're a bunch of troublemakers."

Fergus hugged Kit and Lorelei. "You two are giving me grey hair. I swear to the Goddess if either of you do this kind of shit again, I will hunt you down and make you regret it."

Lorelei patted his back awkwardly. "Okay?"

"I already regret it." Kit gave him a sad look over Fergus's shoulder. "Luca, Ana, Chichi, and Hazelnut?"

"All four made it," Tack answered. "Chichi will be fine with some rest, and Hazelnut is guarding Pearl. Anabelle and Luca were more seriously injured, and there were some complications. We'll know more when we get home."

Kit's lip trembled, and he buried his face in Fergus's neck.

Tack wanted to hold him so badly, but he knew Kit's family had been worried too.

Fergus passed them to Ren and took Kelby. "Ren is going to give you a spanking when we get home."

Kit and Lorelei made identical, disgusted faces, and Tack laughed. *Damn it, I'm even starting to kind of like Lorelei*, he thought.

A few moments later, the corridors were starting to thin out. "We should get to the surface," Tack said, sighing. Exhaustion was pressing him hard. It felt like it had been weeks and not hours since Kit had disappeared.

"Yes, we should." Ren released Kelby, and they started down the corridor. Nerio and Finch met them before they got far.

Nerio's eyes froze on Seamus and Oscar. The boy was still wrapped around Seamus. "The curse?"

"Kit and Tack broke it," Seamus said, hugging Oscar tighter. "They traumatized my new son."

Oscar giggled. "You covered my eyes and pushed me out into the hallway."

"You still know what happened." Seamus shook his head. "Traumatized."

Nerio grabbed Tack, making him yelp. His dad hugged him tight and pressed kisses all over his face. "I can finally hold you, son."

"Dad, calm down." Tack laughed at Ren, Fergus, and Kelby's looks of shock. "The Latch Bay snobs are watching us."

"Fuck 'em." Nerio kissed his forehead. "It looks like you're wounded. We need to get you up to the surface."

"Whoa." Hali swam from the middle corridor, Talia and Kai behind her. "What's going on here?"

Tack watched Kai and Seamus closely. The two were acting stranger than usual.

Seamus swallowed hard, face pale. "The curse is broken."

Kai shook his head and held his hands up. "I can't deal with this. First Sea Witch Marlowe and now you?"

Tack frowned. "What are you talking about?" *Please, Goddess, tell me Kai isn't Seamus's mate.*

"Nothing," Seamus said. "Absolutely nothing. It's cold, and we all need food and rest."

Kit kissed Nerio's cheek, then snuggled into Tack's side. "Let's go home."

CHAPTER 24

They were all gathered in Cyreus's study to celebrate their victory. They had lost people, but far fewer than Tack had expected. The wounded were being treated, and their armies were dispersing and heading home. Ailig, Eades, and all the pirates and mercenaries were dead. Tack called that a job well done.

Hali stuffed another pillow behind Kit's back. "Do you need another sandwich, Kit? What about you, Seamus? Oscar?"

"For the love of the sea, sit down, Hali." Finbar pulled her into a hug. "You've been rushing around since we got back."

"I missed too much." Hali growled. "I didn't get to see Tack act all awkward and stupid as he wooed Kit, damn it. I feel like I'm behind."

"That's not really how it happened," Kit said, laughing.

Tack looked around. "Where's Grandpa?"

"Do you really need to ask?" Finch smirked.

"Good point." Tack shrugged. He knew where he'd prefer to be right now, and Abernathy had more time to make up for than Tack did.

"I can't believe your grandpa mated *my* grandpa," Mabel said, frowning. "In the caverns."

"The sex caverns," Lorelei said, smiling wickedly. She painted another of Kit's toenails orange.

Tack settled his arm around his mate's shoulder and let himself settle into the soft couch. "The doctor checked Kit over. He's alright, and he'll have the baby any day now."

Kelby smiled fondly. "I wish we could be there, darling."

"You can," Nerio said, sighing. "I'd like our kingdoms to be on good terms. My armies could have cleaned the pirate base out, but we would have had far more casualties. We also wouldn't have had the location. We work well together."

Ren nodded. "We do. If you don't mind, we'll stay Coalswell Tides until the baby is born."

Kit rolled his head to the side and smiled. "Thank you, Nerio."

Tack's dad raised his glass to Kit. "You broke our curse, Kit. Thank you."

"I didn't break it," Kit said, yawning. "I never would have been able to if Tack hadn't made me fall in love with him. You raised a sweet son, Nerio."

Finch laughed. "Have you seen him feed people to Lola? It's an actual thing."

Tack tossed a pillow at his friend. "Shut up."

A soft buzz sounded, and Mabel looked surprised. "That's the door. I'll be right back."

"Someone needs to send a plane or helicopter for Dover and the others," Fergus said. "They'll want to be there for Kit too."

Ren typed a message out on his phone. "I've messaged Ervin. He'll see that it's done."

Nerio tensed in his seat. "Shit."

Tack frowned. "What's wrong, Dad?"

The door to the study banged open, and Sea Witch Johanna rushed in, face stricken. "Nerio, why didn't you tell me?"

Nerio stood up. "I'm sorry, Johanna. I didn't know how to go about it. I didn't think you could possibly trust a Muir after what my ancestors did. Why would you even *want* to be my mate?"

"Mate?" Tack sat up, wincing. He wasn't sure how he felt about Johanna being his step-mom.

Johanna shoved Nerio, then grabbed his face and kissed him.

Lorelei groaned. "Not again. Are they going to fuck on the chair now?"

"Lorelei, hush," Kelby hissed.

Tack noticed movement at the door. Sea Witch Marlowe watched Seamus, eyes sad. The man's jet-black hair glittered in the light and bags hung under his eyes, reminding Tack of the Leviathan Johanna claimed lay imprisoned in the Deep. *Guess I wouldn't get much sleep either if I was sitting on top of a Leviathan.*

When Johanna pulled back from the kiss, tears fell down her pale cheeks. "I would love to be your mate,

Nerio. I've watched you for a long time. You're a good man, and I'd give anything to be able to have you."

Nerio's face filled with wonder. "Then, mate me."

"I can't," Johanna said, voice breaking. "We carry our own curse, Nerio. We are a people of the sea *and* the land, but Sea Witch Adriane's hatred took our humanity from us. We live in a dark, sunken city, and no merfolk of the Deep can keep their human form for long. Not a single one of us. Marlowe and I have managed to keep our forms the longest, but it drains our power."

Nerio shook his head. "How do we break the curse?"

Marlowe snorted. "To break our curse, the three kingdoms must each sacrifice their own desires and work together for the greater good. I don't see that happening."

"Nonsense," Ren said, waving his hand. "We can find a volunteer from each kingdom to do something together, maybe build a boat together or harvest clams."

"That's not enough," Johanna said, smiling sadly. "Thank you, Ren, for even considering it. The curse sounds vague but is actually quite specific. The three *must* sacrifice their own desires. Any volunteers would just be doing what they are told. We've tried before by paying merfolk from each kingdom. The curse knows the difference. As for the task, it must be for the greater good of all three kingdoms. That's no easy thing to accomplish."

"If you can't live on land, then I'll come to the

Deep," Nerio said, voice hard. "Tack is ready to lead our kingdom. It's a little earlier than planned, but I don't –"

"No." Johanna cupped Nerio's face again. "I won't allow you to be cursed too. It's hard, Nerio. The land calls us, but we're stuck in the cold depths. It has its own beauty, but it's not the same." Her eyes met Tack's for a moment before returning to Nerio. "I also have responsibilities in the Deep. I... I don't think we *can* be together. I wish things were different, but they are what they are."

Johanna turned away and ran from the room.

"No." Nerio chased after her.

Tack shared a look with Kit. The joy he felt in his mating bond was indescribable. To think that his father would never experience that tore a hole in his heart.

Marlowe cleared his throat and pointed at Oscar. "I actually came here for the child. He's meant to be my apprentice."

Seamus snorted. "I don't think so. I'm not sending Oscar to the Deep to be cursed. He's my son, and he'll stay with me."

Marlowe scowled and stalked toward Seamus. "You can go live with Kai in the warm, shiny castle, but I need my apprentice."

"What does Kai have to do with this?" Talia asked, brow arched.

"Nothing," Kai said, standing. "Seamus and Oscar can both go live with you in the Deep. You can be a family."

"Seamus will stay with you," Marlowe said, glaring at Kai. "He can feed you delicious food until you're as big as a house, and you can have a hundred cute, chubby babies."

Kai stood and poked Marlowe in the chest. "He loves Oscar, and your cold-hearted ass could use some happiness. He'll stay with you, and *you* can have a hundred cute, chubby babies."

Seamus stood up, Oscar's hand in his. "Oscar and I will stay at home, and you two can go fuck yourselves." He pulled Oscar from the room, and Tack could hear them stomp upstairs.

"Look what you did," Marlowe said, crossing his arms. "You think you're so perfect and self-sacrificing, don't you?"

Kai threw his hands up. "I don't even know how to respond to that, Sea Witch Emo."

Marlowe narrowed his eyes. "You had best hope you don't meet me in the water, Prince Shiny." He left the room, and they all heard the front door slam.

Kai kicked the chair beside him, then stormed from the room.

Lorelei shook her head and added a black stripe to Kit's orange toenail. "And everyone says *I'm* full of drama."

CHAPTER 25

*K*it gripped the headboard and groaned as Tack pushed into him from behind. Tack's balls slapped against him with each thrust, and his dick felt like it would explode at any moment.

Tack's teeth bit down on his mating mark, and Kit lost it, shooting cum all over the blankets.

His mate's contented purr rumbled along Kit's back, and Tack sped up his thrusts, angling to ping Kit's prostate with each movement. The feel of Tack's warm cum filling him, made him shiver. Tack's dick was a hell of a lot better than any of Kit's dildos.

Tack helped him settle away from the wet spot on the bed and cuddled him. His big hands smoothed over Kit's belly. "I tried not to think about what your skin would feel like, but I couldn't help it. I could never imagine how soft and warm you are."

"No more sleeping apart." Kit leaned his head back and kissed Tack's chin. "No more gloves or kissy handkerchiefs."

"Nothing between us ever again," Tack whispered against his ear. "I love you, Kit."

The words made him shiver. *Tack loves me. Me!* "I love you too."

A fist pounded on the door. "Hurry it up, you two," Dover yelled. "Esme and Seamus said breakfast is ready, and I'm starving."

"You can eat without us," Kit yelled back.

"Anabelle will be there." Dover sounded smug.

"Damn it," Kit wiggled out of Tack's arms. "I'm glad Anabelle will be okay. I feel so bad."

Tack slid out of bed and pulled on his clothes. "I won't lie to you. It was a foolish decision. However, Anabelle and Luca knew better."

Kit felt tears threaten at Luca's name. *He's alive, and that's the important thing.*

While Anabelle was starting to recover, Luca had a long road to go. He had been shot, stabbed, and beaten while protecting Kit and Pearl. Because of his injuries, he couldn't keep his position in the guard, but he *would* live.

"Daddy, hurry up." Pearl tapped on the door. "Chichi is hungry."

Kit made a face and dressed quickly, pulling on his favorite orange sarong and teal kimono. He slipped his feet into his lobster slippers and paused outside Hazelnut's house.

He tapped on her door, and his fairy friend opened. "I'll bring you more sugar, Hazelnut," he whispered. "How's your girlfriend?"

Another fairy peeked over Hazelnut's shoulder and

blew him a kiss.

Kit chuckled. "I see you two are doing good. I'll make sure you two have a feast."

Tack slipped his boots on. "Esme already assigned one of her staff the duty of bringing a platter of sugar to the woods every morning. Do we really need to bring Hazelnut and Daisy more?"

Kit glared at him. "Of course, we do."

Tack grinned and kissed him, bracing a hand on his belly. "Whatever makes you happy."

"I'd also like to arm the fairies with more than thorns," Kit said as they left the room.

"No," Kai said, shaking his head. "Finch told me what the fairy swarm did. Why would you arm them? What happens when you piss them off?"

"I won't piss them off," Kit said sweetly. "I'm not an asshole like you."

Kai groaned and picked Pearl up, hugging her. "I told you. Marlowe and Seamus need to be together. Marlowe can't leave the Deep, and I can't leave Latch Bay. At least two of us should be happy."

"Martyr." Dover mock coughed into his hand.

"Dumbass." Kit coughed into his own hand.

"You love me, don't you Pearl?" Kai asked, eyes pleading.

Pearl sighed and patted his cheek. "I love you, but you make me tired."

Tack burst into laughter. "That's my girl."

Blueberry stretched on his bed near the window. The dragonling chirped when he saw Kit, running to him.

Chubber watched the dragonling unhappily but didn't protest when Dover picked Blueberry up and handed him to Kit.

"Why do you think Chubber doesn't like Blueberry?" Ben asked. "Otis and Rachael like him well enough."

Kit glared at the chicken perched on his kitchen counter. He was going to have to disinfect everything before he could cook again.

"I don't know," Tack said, rubbing his chin. "Orneriness, maybe? It doesn't seem reasonable to dislike someone you don't really know." He batted his eyes at Kai. "Does it?"

Kai scowled. "I hate you all."

They pestered Kai all the way to the dining room.

Abernathy and Cyreus were already there, holding hands as they stuffed their faces with eggs and bacon.

Hali and Eugenia were already having a drinking contest, one that Eugenia was winning. Again.

"It's not even noon." Kelby tsked. "Eugenia, can you at least try to behave?"

Seamus sat at the kids' table with Oscar and the other children. Earl barked a hello, and Jamie tossed him another herring. Otis barked and ran to Jamie, tongue hanging out. Jamie laughed and gave Ben's dog a bit of bacon. *I really wish I could sit at the kids' table.*

Carina walked around the room, bouncing a fussy Prue in her arms. "You're as loud as your daddy, aren't you?"

Ben looked affronted for a moment. "Oh, wait, you

mean, Dover." He shrugged and went back to his breakfast, ignoring Dover's glare.

"And to think I brought Otis *and* Rachael with me." Dover petted Chubber's head. "Next time, I'm leaving the guard chicken at home."

Blueberry chose that moment to climb over to Dover's shoulder and curl around Chubber.

Dover froze, eyes wide.

Chubber stared at the dragon for a moment, then chirped and patted the dragonling's cheek.

"Please tell me they aren't murdering each other on my shoulders," Dover asked, voice soft.

"Nope." Ben grinned. "They're settling down to sleep. You're going to have a sore neck tonight."

Dover gave Ben a flirty look. "You'll rub it for me, won't you."

Kit wrinkled his nose and ignored his brother.

"Ciao, bella." He stooped to kiss Anabelle's cheek. His guard had a place of honor at the table today, whether she liked it or not.

Petra plumped another pillow and set it behind Anabelle. "I don't know why you're not in bed, recovering."

"Beth missed Pearl, and my wife was driving me insane." Anabelle pouted. "She keeps pampering me."

"Oh, the horror," Finch said, rolling his eyes.

Kit's eyes watered as he stared at the stitches on her face. He hated that he had made a stupid decision that got her hurt. *I need to go visit Luca after breakfast*. He would bring Pearl. Luca adored the girl.

Nerio sat between Ren and Finbar. Both men were

trying their best to distract Tack's dad, but Kit hurt at the pain he saw in Nerio. Johanna had remained adamant about not mating with Nerio and had returned to the Deep.

Pearl slid down from Kai's arms and ran to Nerio. "I'll give you a kiss." Pearl smacked a kiss on Nerio's cheek, then kissed Ren and Finbar's cheeks too.

Tack smiled. "She liked getting rid of the hanky."

Kit smiled, eyes watering. "Me too."

Pearl ran to Seamus and the kids' table. "I'll give you a kiss too." Seamus tickled her before bending to get his kiss. She giggled, then hugged Oscar. "I'll give you kiss *and* hug."

Oscar seemed happy with the attention. Kit eyed him. It had only been a few days, but Oscar's color was already better and he was eating well.

Kelby stood up and helped Tack lower Kit into a chair. "Sit down, dear. Now, have you finally named the baby?"

Kit growled. "No. Nothing seems right."

Fergus cut into his waffle. "What about Casper? I read that it means *master of treasure*. Maybe he'll find his treasure quickly and easily."

Kit looked at Tack. "It's perfect, isn't it?"

Tack leaned down and kissed him. "Fergus is right. Maybe a lucky name will make things easier for him."

KIT GROWLED AS HE PUSHED AGAIN. "WE'RE NAMING THE little fucker Demon. Why. Won't. He. Get. Out?"

Tack wiped a cloth over Kit's forehead. "It's alright. It's alright."

Kit groaned and pushed again. "That's what you've been saying for the last hour. Mother, he's broken."

Kelby patted his hand. "Alphas are useless during labor, darling. Your father always ran around in a panic."

Fergus gave Kit a small sip of water. "Like he's doing right now. Goodness, he really is useless."

"Well, at least Nerio and Finbar are keeping him company," Kelby smirked. "They look like chickens, Kit."

Dover looked up from his magazine when Kit yelled as another contraction hit. He gestured around the full room. "This is why I only had Shauna and Hester with me when I had Prue. At least you left Pearl with Seamus."

Kit gritted his teeth and pushed hard. "This. Is. A. Magical. Motherfucking. Moment."

Lorelei stood next to the doctor, eyes wide in horror. "I'm never having children. It looks like it's going to explode from your omega line."

"It's supposed to look like that," Petra said, eyes glued to Kit's stomach. "Right, doctor?"

"Yes," the doctor said. "If you ladies would step back, I think this boy is ready to come out."

"Oh, Goddess." Lorelei darted across the room, hand covering her mouth.

Kit squeezed his eyes shut and pushed as hard as he could. He felt his demon child slip from him and a second later, he heard a loud cry.

"Finally. Tack, how does he look?" Kit asked. He panted as he looked around. "Tack?"

Fergus sighed. "He fainted. I'll check on him."

"I don't really blame him," Kai said, face pale. "Marlowe and Seamus are both omegas."

"What difference does that make, darling?" Kelby kissed Kit's cheek and started wiping the sweat from his face. "You're not planning on mating them, remember? You're just going to die alone with no one to love you."

Kit chuckled weakly. "I love you, Mother. I even love you better than Shauna. I don't know about Shell, though. She's a really sweet otter. Then there's Petra."

Kelby smacked his arm. "You're horrible."

"What did I miss?" Tack asked, standing up.

Petra chuckled and handed a wiggly, red-faced newborn to Tack. "Just your son being born. Here you go, Otter Daddy."

Tack's eyes filled with tears as he stared at the baby in his arms. He stroked a finger down Casper's cheek. "Kit, look what we made."

Kit smiled, knowing he'd get his turn in a minute. "We made treasure, tesoro mio."

EXCERPT FROM THE SEA WITCH

I hope you enjoyed returning to the world of The Silver Isles. Book Three is titled *The Sea Witch* and will follow Prince Kai, Prince Seamus, and Sea Witch Marlowe's story. Read below for an unedited excerpt:

Marlowe watched the merfolk gather on the beach. He was reluctant to join them in the sun but knew he had no choice. He couldn't stand the dead-eyed woman Johanna had become.

He loved his mentor like a mother, and in most ways, she had been a mother to him from the moment his tentacle tail turned black, declaring him a sea witch. His own parents loved him, but they didn't understand the warm flow of the water in his veins. They didn't hear the song it sang. They didn't feel the menacing evil at the bottom of the Deep.

"For Johanna," he muttered and summoned his legs. The process hurt and pulled at his energy, but it had to be done.

As he walked out of the water, his black sarong fell to cover him. His feet sank into the sand, and he wiggled his toes with each step. *Feet are so odd.*

His mates were on opposite sides of the small bonfire on the island at the edge of the deep. His angry, shiny blade stood with his sister, Talia, and their parents. His soft and sweet flutter of sunshine stood with Kit, Tack, and all the children.

Finbar met him at the waves. "Thank you for coming. I know this is hard."

Marlowe nodded. For some reason, ever since they had met, Marlowe felt an odd sense of kinship with Seamus's father. The man didn't seem to judge him for rejecting Kai and Seamus. In fact, he seemed to understand why Marlowe was doing it. *They won't find happiness with me*, he thought.

Dover and Ben waved as he approached the bonfire. Marlowe scowled. It was so warm, and he hated that he liked it.

"Hey, Marlowe," Ben smiled nervously. "You know Hester, right?"

Ben's hedge witch friend stood beside him. The old woman gave him a knowing look. "We met at Ben's wedding."

"She did a scrying the other day and saw something." Ben shuffled his feet. "I don't pretend to understand her visions, but they've been helpful before."

Marlowe gave her a look. "Johanna said you were exceptionally strong. What did you see?"

Hester grinned. "Everyone get your asses in gear. It's time to fix this problem."

The group gathered closer to the fire.

Tack crossed his arms. "Dad is a mess. He spends most of his time staring out his bedroom window. Now that he knows Johanna would mate with him if she could, he can't think of anything else."

Marlowe bit his lip. "Johanna is just as bad. She always laughs. Always." He frowned. "Now, she just focuses on our duties with no care for anything else. Perch and Dilly don't even cheer her up."

Ren blinked. "Perch and Dilly?"

"Her eel companions," Marlowe said. He narrowed his eyes when Otis sat on his foot. The dog's ears seemed to call to him. "Siren ears."

Ben gave him a puzzled look. "What?"

Marlowe gave in and pet the dog's silky ears. "We need to break the curse, so Johanna can be with Nerio." He eyed Oscar. The boy was playing with Pearl and Shawn under the supervision of Kelby and Carina. "Also, so I can train my apprentice since you insist he live on land."

Seamus smiled. "Good idea. Did you get a plate of food? Of course, you didn't. Everyone started talking. I'll feed you."

Marlowe almost whimpered when his sweet omega went to get him food. Seamus was such a caring person. His ass was also a work of wonder.

He felt Kai's eyes on him and knew his mate had caught him watching Seamus. "It's time all three kingdoms worked together."

ALSO BY C.W. GRAY

The Blue Solace Series – science fiction/fantasy, mpreg

1. The Mercenary's Mate – https://amzn.to/2MAOFEH
2. The General's Mate – https://amzn.to/2G1abRE
3. The Soldier's Mate – https://amzn.to/2S7R6ng
4. The Lieutenant's Mate – https://amzn.to/2THZ47w
5. The Engineer's Mate – https://amzn.to/2HpI4vH
6. The Captain's Mate – https://amzn.to/2knP03W
7. The Rebel's Mate – https://amzn.to/3aadoKH

Charybdis Station – science fiction/fantasy, mpreg, spin-off

1. Death's Mate – *Coming Soon*
2. Rune and Silas – *Coming Soon*
3. Fire's Mate – *Coming Soon*

The Hobson Hills Omegas – non-shifter, mpreg, omegaverse

1. Falling for the Omega – https://amzn.to/2BgWURV
2. Snow Kisses for My Omega – https://amzn.to/2TdDiol
3. Romancing the Omega – https://amzn.to/2UNENKD
4. Healing the Omega – https://amzn.to/2FNcXrY
5. A Pint for my Omega – https://amzn.to/2XItQf7
6. Unraveling the Omega – https://amzn.to/2xRCnRL
7. The Alpha's Christmas Wish – https://amzn.to/2qXkGAl
8. Convincing the Alpha –
9. Book Nine TBA – *Coming Soon*
10. Book Ten TBA – *Coming Soon*

Hobson Hills Shorts – short stories from the world of Hobson Hills Omegas

1. The Beta's Love Song – https://amzn.to/2UrRPNN
2. Bennett's Dream – https://amzn.to/2GwSpG3
3. Justin's Journey – https://amzn.to/2DhW1t1
4. Grey's Gift – https://amzn.to/2BcjxXf
5. Hobson Hills Shorts: Volume One – https://amzn.to/2M3oGGZ

Holiday Omegas Shorts – holiday short stories from the

world of The Silver Isles – paranormal, mpreg

1. Cauldron Cake Pops and a Witch's Kiss – https://amzn.to/33wMrhc
2. Sugar Cookies and a Witch's Love – https://amzn.to/2NE4CeJ
3. Candy Hearts and a Witch's Ring – https://amzn.to/2wtMVcD
4. Carrot Cake and a Witch's Surprise – *Coming Soon*

The Silver Isles – paranormal, mermen, mpreg

1. The Guppy Prince – https://amzn.to/2q9Q8en
2. The Not so Little Merman –
3. The Sea Witch – *Coming Soon*

If you would like to keep up with releases, please like and follow me on Instagram (@c.w._gray) or Facebook (@cwgrayauthor), join C.W. Gray's Reading Nook on Facebook, or visit my website at https://cwgray-author.com.

EXCERPT FROM THE MERCENARY'S MATE

Unedited excerpt from *The Mercenary's Mate* – Book One in the Blue Solace Series

Silverlight System, Planet Vextonar

"Next up is a real gem, gentle folks!" The auctioneer leered toward the large crowd at the bottom of the stage. He was a Betonize-human hybrid, sharp teeth a glaring white. "This little girl's part Prime and part Lower. Don't see that on Vextonar too often."

The crowd's boisterous laughter and cheering filled the room. Eight people had already been auctioned off, and the day was still young. Leti Ando gritted his teeth and awkwardly shuffled his feet. The bulky cast on his lower leg made him slower than normal, and there were too many strangers here, too much movement. He wanted to be in his rooms, reading the new Old-Earth journal he'd gotten his hands on.

Draif shot him a sympathetic look. Leti's best friend

was no less uncomfortable in the auction house but had insisted on coming with him. "You knew it'd be like this, Master," Draif whispered.

Leti glared at his friend, his black eye and busted lip protesting the expression. "I hate it when you call me that."

Draif gave him a small smile, dark eyes on the stage. "I know. Why do you think I do it?" His smile faded. "It's her, Leti."

Leti startled, stumbling and knocking into some of the men around him. He did his best to ignore the grumbles, his heart beating fast in his chest. Monty slipped from his head to his shoulder, and Draif grabbed his arm to steady him. For such a small, slender man, Draif had a strong and sure grip that came in handy when Leti's clumsiness attacked.

Leti ignored the grumbles around him, eyes locked on the stage. A modestly dressed woman stood tall. She held a whimpering, blanket-wrapped bundle in her arms.

"This little lady is up for sale," the Auctioneer said. "She comes from a Prime daddy and his mistress, a Lower woman. Unnamed infant, but good potential. Mommy's dead and Daddy don't want a Lower brat, so there won't be no contest of ownership once she's bought. We'll start bidding at 250? Can I get 250?"

Leti sighed and closed his eyes. "I can't believe Father is selling his own child. I hate that he deals in slavery at all, but his own daughter?"

"Yeah, well, he didn't seem to like your opinion too much last night when you brought it up." Draif grabbed his hand and squeezed. "Not that he needs much excuse to beat the shit out of you. It was the threat to sell you too that worries me the most."

It wasn't appropriate for a bed-slave to hold his master's hand, but the two of them had never been *appropriate*. Nothing was normal about a Prime citizen who didn't have sex with his bed-slave, little less treat him like a slave, and nothing was normal about a bed-slave who was demisexual and had a scarred face and damn good fighting skills.

Draif had been Leti's best friend since they were both fifteen. Leti's father gave him to his son and told him to dominate the "broken" slave and prove himself a man. The arrogant Prime often told his son that he was so fat and awkward that no one would ever want him, especially with his attention always on his studies and research.

Leti might be a breeder male, able to have children, but his father assured him no one would ever offer for him like they would a daughter. And love? According to his father, no one could ever love him, not even some mixed breed alien. Being a breeder male showed his blood was too diluted to be human enough. There was too much Wello blood in his ancestry. Father always blamed Leti's mother for it, but never to her face. He was an arrogant bully, not stupid.

In his father's mind, a bed-slave would guarantee that Leti would at least be a man in the bedroom. Leti tried not to complain too much, though. Draif had proven to be the best thing that ever happened to him. He was his loyal confidant and best friend from the start and soon became his assistant, body guard, and overall jack-of-all-trades.

Where Leti struggled in anything outside of his books and pets, Draif could seemingly master any skill if he set his mind to it. More importantly, though, Leti loved Draif more than anything in all the galaxies. He was his brother in all but blood. His family.

"620 to the Drall in the corner. Can I get 630, anyone? 630?"

"Is your lawyer bidding?" Draif whispered.

Leti looked at his communicator. "Yes. He'll keep topping whatever's offered. She'll be ours in a few minutes."

"You father won't like that, Leti. What are we going to do? We can't hide her in your rooms until she's eighteen. I guess we could put her in Wobble's stable, but who wants to live with an Old-Earth Llama?" Draif paused and eyed his friend. "Well, except for you."

Leti grinned. "When I get her, you are going to take her to the spaceport. Talk with Dottie. She's going to sneak all of us on a random ship going out of the system. Father would be alerted if we used our passports, so we have to sneak, at least at first. Once we're out of the Silverlight system, I can tear up your contract as well as hers. You'll both be free."

Draif squeezed his hand tight. His eyes left the stage, widened in disbelief. "We're leaving the system?"

Leti snorted. "I've given you several chances to leave over the last ten years, but you wouldn't go."

"I couldn't possibly leave you behind. I love you," he said with no hesitancy. "What about your menagerie?"

Draif looked at the vexal newt happily perched on Leti's shoulder. "Monty here wouldn't be a problem, but you can't possibly expect to sneak all of them onboard a ship and I know you won't leave them." Draif shook his head, dumbfounded. "What about money? How will you survive? I can easily get work, but you're a trained historian. They aren't exactly rolling in credits." He paused, already forming a plan. "I could work and you could stay home and take care of the baby. You'd be good at that. You love. It's your thing, and in the end, that's all it really takes. We can figure out how to feed her and change a diaper."

"1050! Can I get 1100? Anyone? 1100?"

"Dottie assures me it will be fine. She's picked out a Drellian cargo vessel and my pets are heading there as we speak, even Wobble." Leti checked his comm, then continued, "As for money, I've been saving for a long time. Do you really think I spend all the credits Father gives me monthly?"

"He's always complaining that you drain his pocket, but I thought he was just being cheap. All you buy are books on your tablet, presents for me, and things for the pets. I think the most expensive thing you bought was the tablet. It came from the Anchor's Rest System, right? Our system is seriously behind on tech."

Leti nodded. "I don't usually use more than a quarter of the allowance. I've been saving my pay from my publications too. It's certainly not much, but I didn't become a historian to make money. I never thought I'd have to." Leti laughed ruefully. "I'm a privileged Prime, right?"

Draif let go of his hand and smacked his arm. "No self-deprecation allowed! We are who we are, there's no changing that. Especially on this world. It's not like you can change castes and become a Worker. Anyways, the gods know that no one deserves to be related to your father or psycho mother." He smiled sadly and nodded toward Leti's broken ankle. "Their love hurts."

Draif looked worried. "Are you going to pack and bring my things too?"

"Of course! Melinda has already started packing for us."

"Will she alert your father?"

Leti checked his comm again. Things were on track. "No. She's the one who urged me to start saving credits when I was twelve. Once we leave, she's going to go to Rothwell and work with her daughter."

"Good." Draif's couldn't seem to stop smiling. "We're really doing this?"

"1520 to the gentleman at the front! 1600 anyone? 1600? Going once. Going twice. Sold to the gentleman in the blue coat!"

Despite his worry, Leti grinned. "Yes. We're really doing this."

Buy Here: My Book

EXCERPT FROM FALLING FOR THE OMEGA

Excerpt from book one in the Hobson Hills Omegas series, *Falling for the Omega*.

Carter loaded the last of his tools into his new work van and shut the door. His first day in his new profession was off to a good start. He had three clients to see today and eight spread out during the rest of the week.

Finally getting his plumbing license had been a good idea, even if his perfect, wealthy family hated the idea of him being a plumber.

Hell, they had also hated the idea of him being a soldier and of him moving out of state when he came back injured. They pretty much hated every decision he made.

The crisp fall wind was cold, but the gold, brown, and red leaves on the trees and ground made the cold worth dealing with. Autumn in Maine sure wasn't the same as autumn in Georgia, but so far, he was damn happy with the move. There was a peace here amongst the trees that he hadn't managed to find anywhere else.

"Hi, Mr. Neighbor!"

A child's voice came from behind him, startling Carter. He spun around, stumbling a bit on his prosthesis, and faced the little girl standing a few feet from his van.

She looked about five or six, with two black braids, caramel skin, and a freckled nose. When she smiled brightly, he saw a small gap between her two front teeth.

A black and gray miniature schnauzer sat at her feet, gaze stern and trained on him.

He looked around and didn't see any adults. His little half acre tract was quite a ways back from the road, nestled between a good-sized apple orchard on one side and a thick forest on the other.

Where the hell had this little girl come from?

"My name's Olive, and I brought you a welcome basket. I made it myself, but Daddy made you one too. He's gonna bring it tonight. I wanted you to get mine first, 'cause it's from me and then we'll be best friends." The little girl paused to take a breath. Her wide brown eyes sparkled and met his straight on, innocent and fearless. "We'll be best friends forever."

She didn't even seem to see the scars along the side of his face. The burn marks had already made two kids cry at the grocery store yesterday. Both times, the parents had been too embarrassed to apologize. They just grabbed their kids and ran.

"Uh, where's your daddy, Olive?" His voice was

deep and cracked, broken by the scarring on his neck. Her adoring stare was starting to freak him out a little. He'd never really been around kids.

"He's at home," she answered and handed him the basket. "See what I brought you? Look, look, look."

"Do you know your phone number? Maybe we could give your daddy a call," Carter said, taking the basket from Olive. He pulled the small hand towel from the top and almost dropped the basket. "Is that a hedgehog?"

"Yep! That's Hodges the hedgehog. He wanted to come visit too. Oh and this is Winston," she said and knelt to pet the small dog.

"Okay, your number?" He tried to keep his gruff voice kind. No sense in scaring the kid.

"Olive! Olive Persephone Wilson! Where are you?" A man's voice called from the orchard, full of panic and desperation.

"Uh oh," Olive said. She hurriedly looked around, then darted behind his van, Winston following her. "That's Daddy." She poked her head out and stared hard. "Tell. Him. Nothing."

She quickly hid again when a young omega rushed out of the orchard. He was her father, had to be. He looked just like her.

Carter suddenly couldn't catch his breath. The man in front of him was simply adorable. He was short and well formed, a little chubby. His black hair fell in curls around his face, and his wide hazel eyes contrasted beautifully with his caramel skin. The same freckles that decorated his daughter's nose, fell across his own.

Where it looked cute on the kid, on her father... Bad thoughts, Carter! Bad thoughts!

"Have you seen a little girl? Black hair? Brown eyes? Miniature schnauzer with her? Maybe a hedgehog?"

Carter stared at the handsome man, mouth gaping, for too long.

The man frowned at him, tilting his head. "Are you alright?" His shy smile revealed the small gap between his front teeth.

Oh fuck, he was so damn perfect. He met Carter's eyes too, didn't even glance at the scars.

"Mister?"

Carter shook his head and did his best to pull himself together. He smiled, as best he could with the scar tissue, and nodded toward the van, holding a finger to his lips, encouraging the man to keep quiet.

Olive's father rolled his eyes and stomped around the van. A squealing Olive ran from her hiding spot and hid behind Carter, hugging him around the waist.

"Mr. Neighbor, save me!" Her giggling told him she wasn't too worried about her father catching her.

"Olive, you scared me to death running off like that." Her father really did look worried. "What have I told you about leaving the house without me?"

"But daddy," she whined. "I wanted to meet Mr. Neighbor. We're best friends now, and I gave him a welcome basket. I was being hospital."

Carter frowned. Hospital?

"Hospitable, baby girl, and it doesn't matter. You are too little to be wandering around by yourself and talking to strangers. No television time this week, and you have to clean out Pooka and Banjo's stalls on Saturday."

Olive gave a big sigh and leaned her forehead into Carter's leg. "Okay, Daddy, but it was worth it. I have a new best friend now."

The man met Carter's stare, a question in his eyes. Carter nodded and gave his best half smile.

"Well, maybe our new neighbor would like to come over for dinner one night? So that we can meet him properly," the man said.

"Yay! Mr. Neighbor, can you come tonight? Daddy's gonna make apple dumplins for dessert."

Carter smiled at the little girl and nodded. "Yeah, if it's okay with your dad."

The man smiled and nodded eagerly. "That would be great. I hardly ever get to cook for anyone but Olive." He gave a flustered look and held out his hand. "Oh, I forgot. My name is Elijah Wilson. I live in the farmhouse with the orchard. Of course, you've met Olive."

Carter shook his hand, touch lingering longer than it should. He was reluctant to release him but finally did. "Yeah, I'm Carter Benson. Just moved here from Georgia."

"Wow, so Maine's probably a bit different, huh?"

"Yeah, but all the colors on the trees? And ya'll actually have snow. I've never seen much of it."

"You say that like snow is a good thing." Elijah shuddered. "Well, welcome to Hobson Hill. I see Olive already gave you a welcome basket."

Carter looked back in it. "There's a hedgehog in

there." His coarse voice was getting rougher as he spoke. He wasn't used to talking so much. Doctors said it was good for him to do though.

"I put cider in there for you. It's in my favorite big girl cup, the one with Moana. There's also butter from Pooka and some of Daddy's bread. It's so yummy!"

"Thanks, Olive. I appreciate it," Carter said. The little girl still hung on his leg, smiling up at him. She was a cute one, he acknowledged, even though she was clearly a little crazy. It was a good crazy though.

"Your alpha won't mind me coming," Carter asked Elijah.

The man winced and lowered his eyes. "I don't have an Alpha, so no, that won't be a problem."

Carter was surprised. Happy, but surprised. This adorable man had to be beating them off with a stick. Of course, some folks thought poorly about single omegas, and some alphas refused to even speak to them. Idiots.

"I guess I'll see you tonight. What time?"

"Oh, is six okay?" Elijah's confidence seemed to bounce back at Carter's question.

"That's fine. I better get to work."

"Yes, of course," Elijah said and pulled Olive off Carter's leg. "Come on, Olive. We better get back to the house. We need to get you to school."

"Okay. Bye, Carter, love you!" The little girl and her dog ran off through the orchard.

"I swear it's exhausting keeping up with her," Elijah sighed. Carter smiled and held the hedgehog out to him. "Thanks," he said, taking Hodges and smiling shyly. "See you tonight. Have a good day at work."

Carter stood frozen as he watched Elijah walk away. He was in trouble. Big, wonderful trouble.

Buy Here: https://amzn.to/2BgWURV

www.ingramcontent.com/pod-product-compliance
Lightning Source LLC
Chambersburg PA
CBHW071748190726
48292CB00003B/904